*Maureen's Do's and Don'ts for
the perfect pretend honeymoon:*

DO:

1. Agree to sleep in separate beds, even if they're only yards apart.

2. Cuddle up to that handsome "groom"—for the photographers, of course!

3. Admire his sexy smile—looking isn't a crime, is it?

DON'T

4. Get lost in soul-stirring kisses.

5. Wish this trip would never end.

6. Fall in love!

Dear Reader,

Boy, did Marie Ferrarella's *Traci on the Spot* bring back a few memories for me. Her heroine is a cartoonist, and she works out the daily dilemmas of her life via her character's escapades. I once dated a cartoonist. However, his character was of the animated-vegetable-saving-the-world variety, and no way would I have wanted to be involved in any of *his* escapades. Of course, maybe if we'd managed to share a night alone in a romantic cabin, I might have changed my mind.

Our second book this month is *First Date: Honeymoon*, by Diane Pershing. Mix together one handsome hero and one waiting-for-Mr.-Right heroine, then add a sham marriage proposal and an equally ersatz honeymoon, and voilà! You've got just the right ingredients for the perfect travel guide to honeymoon bliss, not to mention passion hot enough to melt granite and a couple whose next honeymoon is going to be the very, *very* real variety.

Enjoy both stories, and remember to come back next month for more adventures in meeting, dating—and marrying—Mr. Right.

Yours truly,

Leslie Wainger
Senior Editor and Editorial Coordinator

Please address questions and book requests to:
Silhouette Reader Service
U.S.: 3010 Walden Ave., P.O. Box 1325, Buffalo, NY 14269
Canadian: P.O. Box 609, Fort Erie, Ont. L2A 5X3

DIANE PERSHING

First Date: Honeymoon

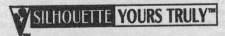

Published by Silhouette Books
America's Publisher of Contemporary Romance

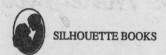

SILHOUETTE BOOKS

ISBN 0-373-52040-9

FIRST DATE: HONEYMOON

About the author

I cannot remember a time when I didn't have my nose buried in a book. As a child, I would cheat the bedtime curfew by snuggling under the covers with my teddy bear, a flashlight and a forbidden (read "grown-up") novel. My mom warned me that I would ruin my eyes, but so far, they still work.

First Date: Honeymoon combines several of my favorite pastimes with the "if onlys" and "what ifs" that thrash about in my mind: two completely incompatible people thrown together; a free spirit versus a control freak; the gypsy in my soul; an enduring love of London and Venice; and an absolute *adoration* of fine food. Heaven, sheer heaven.

I live in Los Angeles, but I'm not in the least affected, promise. My two children, Morgan Rose and Ben, are both in college, and I enjoy a fun career as a voice-over performer. I'm blessed by a second career as a writer, having published several romance novels in the past three years. This is my first for Silhouette, and I want to thank them for letting me vent my sense of humor. Hey, I'm easy; if you laugh at my jokes, I'm yours forever.

Diane Pershing

To my foreign advisors, Stu, Brenda, Aunt Pearl,
Ettore, Luana and Federico—and to
Jill Marie Landis for a plot twist. Thanks.

1

"**H**i, Carla! Great day, huh?" Mo waved at the dark-skinned woman behind the counter.

"Afternoon, Mo. In a hurry, I see. For a change." This last was said sardonically, and Mo grinned at the woman as she dashed past, heading for the post-office boxes. Row upon row of small locked compartments lined the walls. When Mo got to number 747, she dug around in her oversize purse.

"Now, where did I put that key?" she muttered to herself, kneeling as she heaved the huge bag from over her shoulder and plopped it onto the marble floor. She had promised herself she would put the key in *one* place so she'd always know where to find it. And she had. But she couldn't remember where that one place was.

Sighing, she began to unload the purse's contents onto the floor, trying not to get in the way of other box holders at this busy San Francisco post office. Wallet, sunglasses, half a bagel, pink baseball cap, a small notebook with Barney on the cover, scrunchies and ribbons and rubber bands.

These were followed by a checkbook with a distressingly low balance, a cotton wraparound skirt to put over her shorts for her interview later, a small stuffed panda with a missing ear that she'd promised her nephew she'd repair, gas receipts, gum, a half-empty box of Good & Plenty, a dented can of cat food that her mother had asked her to return to the market. Finally, at the bottom of the bag, in a package of striped birthday candles, she found her round gold post-office box key.

"Aha!" Mo said in triumph. After putting the key ring over her pinkie and hurriedly stuffing everything else back into the purse, she stood up and slung the bag over her shoulder.

Mo opened her mailbox and removed several mail-order catalogs, which she jammed into her purse for later perusing. She'd been hoping for some positive responses to the résumés she'd sent out—she'd been out of work for a month—but the only other object in the box was a thick, oversize envelope. She tore it open, extracted and unfolded several sheets of paper.

What seemed to be a booklet of tickets dropped to the ground. She bent over to retrieve them. Airline tickets, she saw as she straightened up. Round-trip, first-class tickets. To Europe.

Mo felt her heart accelerate as she clutched the booklet in her hand. Europe—the dream, daily and nightly, since she could remember.

Quickly, she skimmed the papers. It seemed to be some sort of itinerary, with the departure from San Francisco scheduled for the following evening, a Sunday. Her eyes scanned the first sheet, then the second. Two weeks. Five cities. Ending up in—could it be?—Budapest! On, of all days, June eighteenth!

Hugging the itinerary and the tickets to her chest, Mo closed her eyes, her rapid heartbeat thumping loudly in her ears. Was it possible? Was this a sign? No, beyond a sign. A miracle?

Reason nibbled at her whirling brain. She tried to ig

nore it, but it kept pecking at her like an insistent bird; reason had a way of doing that. With great reluctance, Mo opened her eyes and forced herself to look more closely at exactly what it was she was holding.

First she read the name on the envelope.

Matthew Vining.

Then the names on the itinerary and tickets.

Mr. and Mrs. Matthew Vining.

Mo sighed loudly. It was no miracle at all.

"Of course," she muttered, her high mood plummeting like the sawed-off upper branch of a redwood tree.

Matthew Vining, the drop-dead gorgeous restaurant reviewer and host of the syndicated radio show "Dining With Vining," had the post-office box next to hers; she'd received his mail by mistake a couple of other times. So then, that's what this was, a mistake. Not a sign, and certainly not a miracle.

Oh, well, she thought. Oh, well. It had been nice to get this close, anyway, even if only for a couple of moments.

She stuffed the papers back into the envelope and was about to hand it to someone behind the service window, when a thought struck her.

Tomorrow. The trip was for the very next day. What if Matthew Vining didn't get to the post office in time? What if something last-minute happened and he didn't collect his tickets? That would be terrible. To ruin an incredible, fantastic trip like that because the post office messed up.

His show originated at KCAW, she knew that, and KCAW's studios were just around the corner. Mo would do a good deed; she would deliver the tickets in person. In any case, it was the proper thing to do, as she'd thoughtlessly ripped open the envelope without first checking who it was addressed to.

Suffused with the spirit of noble generosity, Mo shoved the envelope into the black hole she called a purse, waved a quick goodbye to Carla and dashed out the door.

Matthew Vining was not happy. In fact, he was extremely annoyed. He stood in the reception area of radio station KCAW, staring at his fiancée. His fists were clenched with tension and his frown was deep.

"I'm not sure I understand, Kay," he said tightly.

"I'm sorry," Kay said, "but this is the right thing to do."

"You're calling off our engagement? You're canceling the wedding? And the honeymoon?"

"Yes," Kay replied in her usual measured, reasonable way. "It simply won't work. We don't love each other."

"But how can you do this? I mean, it's tomorrow." They were momentarily alone—the receptionist was on a break and things always quieted down at lunchtime— but Matt matched Kay's even tone. They never raised their voices to each other. "What will happen?"

"As I'm the one causing the problem, I'll take care of all the details."

"Yes, but—" He groped for something to say, anything that might salvage this impossible turn of events. "We get along so well."

"Do we?"

"Of course we do. We're so compatible. We read the same magazines, like the same films...." Not to mention the fact that Kay was an organized person, and not given to emotional outbursts. Two very good reasons why he'd been attracted to her in the first place. "You're exactly the kind of wife I want."

She stared at him, her normally placid expression overlaid with a hint of—what? Sadness. Even regret. "There's a difference between the kind of wife you want and the woman you want for your wife," she said gently. "It's not enough, Matthew. I thought it would be, but it's not."

His heartbeat sped up with panic. "But what about the book? I mean, I have a contract to write a book about my honeymoon." He kept the volume down, but he actually felt like shouting right about now. "Everything's set—hotel reservations, photographers, the cable TV—show contract. How the hell will I be able to write the book now?"

Kay's expression lost its sadness; in its place was a bitter little smile. "I was right."

She removed the diamond ring from the third finger of her left hand and dropped it into his suit pocket, making sure to pat the wrinkles out after she did. Then she gazed into his eyes one last time, nodded and said, "Have a nice career, Matt." With that, she walked out the double glass doors of the reception area.

Matt stood staring after her for what seemed like hours, but was probably no more than half a minute. His hands remained in fists at his side and his heart thudded insistently. He was shocked. Shocked speechless. Not, interestingly, at the thought of losing Kay, although that was bad enough. No, it was more that he could almost hear the walls of his carefully built career tumbling down around him, and that thought was unbearable.

A phone rang four times, then someone from one of the offices must have picked it up because the ringing stopped. Over the speakers, Matt could hear the voices of the talk-radio show that was on the air live. A woman was whining about her husband and the host was soothing her with the usual psychobabble pabulum. As though from a distance, Matt wondered when his thought process would get in gear again and when he would move from his frozen position.

Then the reception area's double doors burst open and a small bombshell came blasting through.

"Oh, goody," she said. "You're here."

"Huh?"

She was young, mid-twenties, he guessed. With the part of him that wasn't still reeling from Kay's announcement, Matt observed that the newcomer had a wild mane of red-gold hair, its thick curls reaching halfway down her back.

"I have something for you, Mr. Vining," said the young woman, setting an enormous purse on the beige carpet and kneeling beside it. She proceeded to unload the most amazing clutter he'd ever seen. Books and food and clothing and a can of cat food.

"Excuse me," Matt said. "I don't think you ought to—"

She interrupted him with a triumphant "I know where it is!," and produced a thick envelope from a side pocket. "This was put in my post-office box by accident. It belongs to you."

Still on her knees, she hugged the envelope to her chest and gazed up at him. She had the most incredibly large blue eyes, the color of cornflowers. At the moment, they were brimming with tears. With the back of her hand, she swiped at the moisture impatiently and, even though her luscious lower lip trembled, managed a shaky smile. Her teeth were small and straight and very white.

"Sorry," she said. "I didn't mean to get all teary there."

Again, Matt did and said nothing. She rose, brushed off her knees and handed the crumpled envelope to him. She wasn't tall, he noted, but her body was perfectly proportioned with drop-dead curves. Slowly, he took the envelope but kept staring at her.

"I'm a little emotional," she said. "You see, I thought my *nagyanya* had sent a sign, but I guess she didn't."

"*Nagyanya?*" Matt managed to say. He peered into the envelope, barely registering its contents, then stuffed the whole thing into his inside suit pocket and shifted his attention to his visitor. He had the feeling he'd been dropped into someone else's dream. "Sign?"

She nodded. "My grandmother. She's gone now, but she lived with us when I was little. Anyway, Great-grandma, that's *Nagyanya's* mother, she had a hot affair with a Gypsy while her husband was off fighting in some war and that's why *Nagyanya* had the sight. She used to tell me stories and read the tarot cards, and one day she said, '*Kis macska*, in your twenty-eighth year...'"

She stopped and laughed. "Sorry. When I try to imitate my grandmother, I wind up sounding like Zsa Zsa Gabor underwater. Anyhow," she went on in her natural voice, a melodic, clear tone, the words tumbling over one another like a fast-moving stream over pebbles, "*Nagyanya* said that in my twenty-eighth year I would meet a man with silver eyes on the banks of the Danube, and he would be my love for life. She was real clear about the silver eyes and the Danube." Breaking off her enthusiastic recital, she wrinkled her nose sheepishly. "Kind of silly, huh."

"Kind of," he agreed. Matt was usually not at a loss

for words, but this woman was reducing him to speechlessness, much as Kay had moments before.

She wore what seemed to be a magenta halter top under a see-through polka-dot-patterned blouse, tied at the waist. Her lime-green shorts—not tight, but not loose either—revealed long, shapely legs. On her feet were leather sandals with straps that wound halfway up her calf. One of those free-spirit types; there were more colors in her outfit than in any Impressionist painting Matt had ever seen.

"Would you care to sit down?" Not sure just why he'd said that, he motioned to one of the beige tweed couches that were set about the large room at various angles.

"Oh, no thanks. I have to get going."

Just then, the door opened and a silvered-haired man hurried through, nodding briskly. "Matt."

"Tim," Matt answered. After the station manager disappeared behind the door leading to the offices and studios, Matt turned to the woman. "But what were you saying about something being a sign?"

"Oh, yes. Well—" she cocked a hip against the edge of the receptionist's unoccupied desk "—I'm twenty-seven, which means I'm in my twenty-eighth year, right? And as they say, time's a-fleeting. I've been trying to save enough money to go to Europe, but, well, Tom— he's my brother, well, one of my brothers—he needed a second car. I mean, with all the kids, you know, it's not fair. Anyway, I lent him the money, and he'll pay me back, he always does, my family's real good about that. But, I guess not before my birthday."

"Which is?"

"In two weeks." She spread her hands. "Get it? In two weeks I begin my twenty-ninth year, and when I opened my mailbox and saw the tickets, and that the last stop on the trip is Budapest—home of the Danube—on my birthday, well, I mean, how could I *not* think it was a sign that the silver-eyed man was, maybe, more than a, you know, bedtime story?"

She grinned, the rosy color of her lips unaided by lipstick, Matt noticed.

"You see?" she said, then shrugged. "Oh, well. I guess it's silly to get your hopes too high, especially at a free trip that comes out of nowhere. Listen, have a nice time, you and Mrs. Vining. I really have to get a move on."

She pushed herself away from the desk and was halfway toward the door, when Matt said, "Wait."

She stopped and turned to him, her eyebrows raised in inquiry.

"Your, uh, purse."

"Oh." She put her hand over her mouth. "I'm sorry. I'm not usually this forgetful. Well, actually, I am." She was on her knees, throwing everything back into the bag before he could offer to help. Standing up again, she slung the purse strap over her shoulder—Matt thought the bag might weigh nearly as much as she did—and said sheepishly, "It seems like I've been working all my life at being more organized, but it hasn't happened yet. I'm considering prayer."

"It can't hurt, I suppose," he said distractedly.

"Well, goodbye again." She headed back toward the door.

"Wait," he said one more time, and she turned again, her hand on the knob. "Who are you?"

Her hand flew to her mouth once more. "Oh, I'm sorry. I know who you are, of course. Matthew Vining.

I've seen your picture on the back of the bus, you know, advertising your show—''

Matt winced. He'd hated that campaign; he'd felt like a sleazy tabloid subject instead of a serious culinary expert.

"And my mom listens religiously to your program," she rattled on. "She likes to fantasize that she's actually eating all that fancy food you talk about, so I feel like I know you. I'm Mo."

"Mo?"

"Maureen, actually. Czerny. That's C-Z-E-R-N-Y."

"Well, Maureen—"

"Mo, please."

"All right. Mo."

"And are you Matthew or Matt?"

"Either," he said, preoccupied with something entirely different from names.

His brain had begun to function again. An idea was forming rapidly and furiously in there, and a list of requirements to make the idea work was forming right along with it. Tunneling his fingers through his hair, he walked over to the desk, thought a moment more, nodded to himself, then half sat on the edge, near the very spot occupied by this Maureen woman moments earlier.

He looked up and met her openly curious gaze. "Would you mind answering a couple of questions?" he asked.

"Questions?" She cocked her head to one side. "What kind of questions?"

"Such as, are you employed?"

"Not at the moment."

"What is your career?"

"Uh, not much of anything, really. A little of this and a little of that."

"Are you encumbered? Husband? Children?"

"Nope."

"Do you have a reference or two that I could call? Um, let's see. Good health and a good constitution, and a minimum of allergies?"

"Hold it just a minute," Mo said, looking perplexed. "Am I being considered for something weird here? What's going on?"

Suddenly, the double doors opened with a bang, and a crowd of returning employees came through, chattering and laughing. The noise and bustle was as annoying as it was unexpected.

Matt pushed himself away from the desk and walked over to Mo. "Come on," he said. "Let's get out of here."

"Excuse me?"

"I would like to buy you a cup of coffee. All right?"

Puzzlement wrinkled her forehead as she pointed her thumb at the door. "Well, but... Uh, I have to go. A job interview. I mean, I need to change into a skirt and—"

"Give me twenty minutes." He grasped her gently by the elbow and smiled at her. "Please. A half hour, tops. Maybe you won't need to go on that interview."

2

It was the smile that did it, Mo thought as they hurried along the sunny, bustling North Beach street. There'd been nothing, zip, not a hint of warmth from Matt Vining until then. What he'd done was mostly frown and stare at her, stoney-faced, from the moment she'd entered the reception area. She'd thought him cold, even arrogant.

Oh, sure, his looks were incredible. Rugged, really, with his jet-black hair, longish and styled by an expert, the olive skin, the richly dark brown eyes under thick, fierce eyebrows. His picture on the bus hadn't done justice to his slightly crooked, masculine nose, the high cheekbones and the way his mouth formed into a stern, we-are-not-amused line.

He was quite tall and well-built and, she imagined, had to come from money; he seemed so at home in his perfectly tailored navy pin-striped suit and soft gray shirt and tie that were clearly not sale items at a discount department store. But Mo had never been a fan of great-looking men, or wealthy men, or famous men. No, she usually went for more offbeat, oddball guys. Matt Vining was definitely not her type.

And then he'd taken her arm and turned that amazing smile on her. Boy, what that change in the angle of his mouth did to his face! Lifted it, lightened it. Warmed him up, made him human, accessible. Younger, too. The smile was slow and kind of lazy...and very, very sexy. It made her think of hot nights and rumpled bedsheets.

So, here she was with Matt Vining in one of San Francisco's hundreds of coffeehouses. In the background, Paul Simon sang softly about being crazy as Matt settled Mo into a ladder-back wooden chair at a small corner table, away from the rest of the customers.

"Hungry?" he asked her.

As a matter of fact, Mo hadn't eaten breakfast that morning. "I could use a doughnut, I guess."

"And how does a caffè latte sound?"

"Whatever name you give it," she said, "just make it hot with lots of cream."

He turned that charming smile on her again and went over to the counter. Like the way he talked, he moved with easy, graceful assurance, as though he knew where he was going and also knew he would be accepted when he got there. You couldn't buy that, Mo thought, and it would be hard to learn. The man had self-confidence and class. Pure and simple.

The diametric opposite of her and her family. The Czernys and the O'Tooles were from good, hardworking peasant stock, unpretentious and down-to-earth, with a little music and magic thrown in. Not a speck of class in any of them—and she was crazy about the whole clan.

She dragged her concentration back to the matter at hand. Why had she been invited here? A job offer? Maybe to house-sit or care for his pets, or maybe even his kids, if he had some. What did Matt Vining want of her?

And why was she ready to say yes, whatever it was?

That one brought her up short. Cut it out, she told herself, turning her attention to the nearby window and gazing out on the passing parade. He was a married man. It was perfectly permissible, she told herself, to be *slightly* turned on by someone who belonged to someone else, as long as she kept it to herself.

"Brioche, scone or biscotti?"

Mo whipped her head around. Matt stood by the table, a plateful of foreign-looking goodies in his hand. She stared at them, then at him. "You pick it."

"The bitter-chocolate biscotti, I think," he said, taking a couple of long crescent-shaped cookies from the plate and setting them on napkins in front of her. Then he returned the plate to the counter and brought back their coffees. Lowering himself onto the chair opposite hers, he took a sip, then nodded. "This place really knows how to make coffee," he said, his rich baritone registering approval. "Their beans are shipped in from Antigua."

"That's nice."

Mo tasted her coffee. It was good, she supposed, but hey, coffee was coffee. She took a bite of her biscotti. It was certainly tasty, but she preferred apple fritters from Winchell's. She didn't say so, though. After all, she was in the presence of a famous Food Expert.

Matt took another sip of his coffee then set the cup down. "So."

"So," she agreed, and waited for him to continue.

When he didn't right away, she wondered why. Suddenly, she was struck with the thought that underneath his smooth exterior, Matt Vining was actually uncomfortable. Mr. Smooth with an attack of nerves?

"What did you want to talk to me about?" she asked brightly, hoping to help things along.

Propping an elbow on the back of his chair, he leaned back and gazed at her for a few moments before giving her a tentative half smile. "I have a little proposition for you."

Mo froze in place, then closed her eyes and counted to ten. Not him, not Matt Vining. Since puberty, she'd been the target of lewd comments and indecent suggestions from way too many males of the species. One of whom was obviously sitting across from her right now.

And her antennae hadn't been working, because she certainly hadn't seen it coming.

Mo lifted her purse strap from the back of her chair and stood. "I'm not interested," she said.

"But you haven't heard my proposition yet."

Slinging the bag over her shoulder, she rested her knuckles on a hip. "You have a new way of saying 'Let's go to bed'?"

Matt seemed startled, then his face creased into a broad grin. Shaking his head, he chuckled. "Sit down. Please. That's not what I meant at all."

"Wasn't it?"

"Scout's honor," he said wryly. "Please, sit down."

Mo did, although at the edge of her chair, ready to take off at a millisecond's notice.

"Look," he said, "this is…business, really. Nothing to do with, well, sex. No," Matt said, more firmly now. "Nothing to do with that."

Oh, Mo thought, aware that she was actually disappointed by his vehemence. Talk about double standards. Protesting when she thought the man was coming on to her, and then feeling let down when he didn't.

Okay, she admitted to herself, okay, so she was a little attracted to him. But only a little. It had been a long time for her. Call her crazy, but men whose soulful brown eyes made her think of thick rugs in front of crackling fireplaces tended to get her blood flowing.

Behave, she told herself. Put a leash on the fantasies.

Moving away from the edge of her chair, she sat up straight and folded her hands on the table. Business, he'd claimed, and business he'd get. "All right," she said reasonably. "Let's hear your proposition."

"It's a little complicated, but the bottom line is..." He paused, then shrugged and said simply, "I need a wife."

"You need a—? But don't you already have one?"

"I would have had one tomorrow. I mean..." He paused again and frowned, then went on crisply, "I was supposed to get married tomorrow and take off on the honeymoon tomorrow night."

"Yes?"

"But just before you came to the station, my, uh, fiancée..."

Matt swallowed. Something in him rebelled against completing the sentence, *My fiancée dumped me.* Instead, he came out with, "My fiancée and I decided to call it a day."

Liar, he thought. Kay had been the one to break it off, but for some reason, he'd been unwilling to say that to Mo. Pride, he supposed. It wasn't easy being rejected, or announcing the fact. Or maybe he was trying to avoid being the recipient of one of those pitying looks that women always gave at these moments.

He might as well have told the truth. Mo's expression was imbued with soft, gentle compassion. "I'm so sorry," she said. "You must feel awful."

He waved it away. "Don't. It's all right. Really. But the thing is, it puts me in a bind. I have this contract for a new book—"

"Good!" she interrupted. "Writing a book will help you forget your pain."

Clearly, she didn't understand. "What I mean is—"

He was interrupted once again, this time by the looming presence of a large woman—her sensible walking shoes, cotton skirt, sunglasses and camera hanging from her neck practically screamed, "Tourist!"—who tapped Mo on the shoulder.

"Excuse me?" the woman said with a thick Southern accent.

"Yes?" Mo said.

The woman was joined by what seemed to be the husband and two teenagers, one of whom was pushing a stroller containing a young child with strawberry-jam smears all around his mouth. The family introduced themselves as the Salingers from Savannah, then Mrs. Salinger produced a city map of San Francisco and showed it to Mo. "We're tryin' to find out where they have those seals, you know, the ones that sit on those rocks and visit with each other?"

"Oh," Mo said with delight. "You mean up at the tip of Golden Gate Park, near Point Lobos. It's not real close—we're on the Bay side. Here, let me show you."

For the next ten minutes, Mo and the family—who pulled up chairs to the small table at Mo's invitation—discussed directions to various venues on BART, where to find the best clothing bargains, the spiciest and most authentic Chinese food, how to get the ferry to Tiburón and the best routes to the Redwoods and the wine country. Matt was asked to contribute, but, except for ideas on which restaurants to frequent, left all the advice-giving to Mo. Mo admired the lady's bracelet, the lady admired Mo's blouse, and all had a generally friendly, person-to-person good ol' time.

Except for Matt. All he could think about was if he was making a major mistake. Was there possibly some other option he could come up with? Surely there was *someone* else...wasn't there? He mentally flipped through his address book, desperately searching for a name that would announce its suitability, but for the life of him, he couldn't think of one woman he knew well enough to ask, or he could imagine tolerating for too long.

No, it would have to be this gregarious, emotional Maureen Czerny...if she went for it. Desperate times, he told himself, called for outrageous measures.

He wished they'd all stop talking. Apart from the fact that, despite his small amount of fame, he never felt comfortable being accosted by strangers, he really needed to get Mo's attention back to their discussion. The seconds were ticking away. It was deadline time.

Still, one, nonanxious part of his mind admitted to a reluctant admiration of Mo and her lively personality. She was a people person, with a kind of glow about her that made others light up, as though in her reflection.

He knew he appeared more standoffish. He'd been a shy child, not unloved but often ignored, and had moved around a lot in his younger life. Later, as a scholarship student at several exclusive schools, he'd come in contact with social snobbery and had developed calluses in the area of interpersonal relationships.

He heaved an inward sigh of relief when the Salingers bid warm goodbyes to Mo, polite nods to him, and exited. The family waved one more time through the storefront window. Then Mo turned to him. "Nice people, weren't they?"

"Salt of the earth," he agreed. "Now, about—"

"Your book!" she said enthusiastically. "I bet it'll be terrific."

"If it gets written." He pulled his chair in closer and

leaned his elbows on the table. "I have quite a lot riding on it. My career, to be exact. I'm trying to expand out of the purely local market, to become more, well, nationally well-known."

"Really?"

He nodded. "The book is to be a guide to romantic eating places and hotels. I'm to review five of the best restaurants in Europe—"

"That sounds like fun," Mo interjected with enthusiasm.

"Yes, but the book's slant—the selling point—is that it's about my honeymoon trip. You see? It will include all kinds of other information for newlyweds—you know, after-hour clubs, unusual shops, jewelry stores. Romantic views, private picnic spots. Out-of-the-way, uh, alcoves for, well, doing what you do on a honeymoon."

A faint blush made Mo's cheeks pink, and she picked up her biscotti. "I see." She took a bite and chewed thoughtfully.

Matt leaned in a little more. "Maybe you don't. There are supposed to be pictures of me and my bride. The book jacket will say something like, 'Matt Vining and his wife show all the ways to celebrate just-married romance on the most romantic continent in the world.'"

He stopped and met her clear, blue-eyed gaze. "The problem is, there *is* no book…if I go on my honeymoon alone. So, I need a wife. Well, a pretend wife. You, I hope."

Mo seemed about to take another bite of her biscotti when his offer registered. Frowning, she stared at him, chewing on one corner of her bottom lip instead of the cookie, which she returned to the napkin. He could see her taking in what he'd said and working it over in that active little mind of hers.

Matt watched Mo's face for her reaction. At least she didn't seem about to get up and leave, for which he was profoundly grateful, so he pressed home his advantage. "You need to get to the Danube by—when?"

"The day before my birthday," she said slowly. "The eighteenth."

"Perhaps your grandmother did send you a sign," he said, not believing it for a minute, but willing to make use of whatever was at hand. "And now you can take advantage of it, make it happen."

Wondering if he was pushing too hard, Matt made himself sit back in his chair. "There'll be a photographer in each city, and a certain amount of, well, fuss made over me and my bride, but I'll try to keep it to a minimum. Of course, there won't be an actual wedding picture because there won't be an actual wedding, but I'll come up with something later, after the trip is over and the book is written. Something about a divorce or an illness." He smiled self-consciously. "I'm making up a lot of this as we go along, but it will work out, you have my word."

"I see."

He waited for something more from her, but she sat, for once, unmoving. He thought of suggesting a percentage of the royalties, but decided not to get too carried away, not just yet. If she needed persuading, maybe he would throw that in. Again, he tried to gauge her reaction, but all he could tell was that he'd stunned her.

He plowed ahead with as much conviction as he could muster. "Frankly, it makes sense to me. You'll get to go all over Europe, fulfill a childhood prediction, and—" he gave her what he hoped was a relaxed, ingratiating smile "—dining alone is depressing. Say you'll do it."

She chewed the other corner of her bottom lip. "Why me?"

The question took him by surprise, but he decided to state the truth. "I'm really not sure, except it has something to do with you being there at the moment I needed you. I would ask someone else, if there were someone else to ask. But I don't have many female friends, and not a lot of people can just pick up and leave with one day's notice. When you came into the station, well, it seemed..." He shrugged.

"Like it was meant to be." Mo finished Matt's sentence, nodding slowly as the full impact of what he was offering hit her. "And the silver-eyed man..."

She let that sentence trail off dreamily in her head. Then she shivered. *Nagyanya* had come through, after all. Mo could feel all kinds of tingling excitement building up in her nerve endings and gathering in her chest. She wanted to sing, to shout, to shower Matt's face with grateful kisses.

But not yet, reason cautioned. Not quite yet.

"So, you'll do it?"

Matt's voice broke into her reverie and she blinked and met his gaze. He was still trying to hide it, but she could tell he was anxious about this, more anxious than he wanted to let on. She imagined he was just heartbroken, and was having an I'll-tough-it-out type of male reaction. Poor man.

"How would we work the money?" she asked. "I'd have to pay my way. I'd insist on that. Afterward, I mean, when I get a job. In installments. I wouldn't feel right otherwise."

"Don't even think of it," he said abruptly.

"But—"

"You're doing me a great favor and the publisher is paying for the whole thing."

"But I—"

"Not another word. Please. Consider it a closed subject."

He was back to the arrogant Matt, the one in control, and part of her wanted to keep on arguing with him just to see if she could get a rise out of him.

But there were other, more pressing details to clear up. Shrugging, she said, "Well, okay. If the publishers are paying."

"So," Matt said. "Can we consider this settled?"

She didn't answer, too busy trying to gather her chaotic thoughts. When making plans, Mo often forgot one or two crucial things. She wanted this time to be different.

"Let's see," she said. "I have no job, so I wouldn't have to give notice." Concentrating hard, she counted off on her fingers. "I could ask Mom to feed the parrot and the duck, but she can't stand the snake. Maybe one of my nephews would do that. I have a passport—it's never been used, but it's up-to-date. I've been prepared for years."

His eyebrows arched in surprise, then he nodded. "Well, good. You'll need a smaller purse and comfortable shoes."

"Will I?"

"We'll be walking a lot."

"Goody. I love to walk." Her forehead wrinkled. "If I go, that is. Let me see, what else?"

She gazed directly at him for a moment, and considered what she knew about him. Not a lot, really; they were strangers. But she could usually tell about people right away, and she knew instinctively she'd be safe with him.

She closed her eyes and let her mind drift. Now was not the time to be her usual impetuous self; this kind of thing shouldn't be decided too quickly.

Matt drummed his fingers on the table. *Please,* he said silently. *Do this.* He waited for her answer, wondering what was going on in that hopscotching brain. He'd just decided that Mo had gone into some kind of trance in the middle of the coffeehouse, when she opened her eyes again. He was treated to yet another of her quicksilver mood changes. Her eyes shone brightly with tears brimming behind her lower lashes.

"This is like something out of a dream," she said softly.

"The trip?"

"The envelope in my mailbox, the offer, the conversation, all of it."

"Do you cry a lot?"

"Sometimes. Yes. When I'm moved, I guess. Don't you?"

"No." He felt his back teeth clenching. He really needed an answer, but he had a feeling that no one ever made Mo's mind up for her. "Are there any questions I can answer?" he said, swallowing his impatience. "Anything I can do to help you decide?"

She steepled her fingers and rested them against her mouth. "If I go—"

"Yes?"

"We'd need to set some ground rules."

"Certainly."

She seemed to be struggling with embarrassment. That face of hers registered everything, Matt thought. You would never have to wonder what she was thinking—it was all out there.

Finally, Mo lowered her hands, lifted her beautifully rounded chin and met his gaze straight on, her large blue eyes wide and serious. "I'm willing to pretend to be your wife, in public. But pretend is all. I expect the relationship to be platonic. I mean, separate bedrooms. Okay?"

"Of course," Matt said stiffly. "I thought that was understood. We're booked into the honeymoon suite at all the hotels. There'll always be a sitting room and a bedroom. I'll sleep on the couch. There will be no problem, I assure you."

It was a perfectly reasonable request, Matt thought silently, and one he would have no trouble honoring. No, Mo might have a buoyant personality and a body to die for, but she was the furthest thing from the serene, capable kind of woman he usually found attractive. They'd just met, but it seemed to him that Mo talked too fast, was scatterbrained and disorganized, and had mood swings that could be written up in medical journals. In other words, his own worst nightmare.

Hands off? Gladly. It would make the trip easier, less fraught with tension.

Why, Mo might even be an asset, he thought generously. Unlike him, she was an unmistakable romantic, with her easy tears and silly tales of silver-eyed men on riverbanks. She obviously liked to talk to people and people liked to talk to her; he could turn that intrusive habit into an advantage. Yes. He would take care of the nuts and bolts of the book—the dining, the accommodations—but it would take someone both gregarious and sentimental, someone like Mo, to sniff out the unconventional, interesting places he would need to fill in the pages.

One might even say that running into her this way was good luck.

A sign, she would say.

"Matt? Hello, Matt?"

Damn. Mo had been speaking, and he'd been off wool-gathering. "Yes?"

"I'll do it."

A moment passed before he said, in an easy and relaxed manner, "Good. I'm pleased."

But deep down inside, in that subterranean, subliminal place where both demons and passions reside—a place not heard from for many years—he could just make out a little voice saying, "Yippee!"

3

Matt paced the area near the international departures gate. For the fifteenth time in as many minutes, he tried to tamp down the nervous excitement he was experiencing while waiting for Mo. Excitement wasn't really the word; it was more a mix of dread, exhilaration and terror, all of which were more volatile emotions than he was used to feeling. But feel them he did.

Asking a complete stranger to pose as his wife! Was he nuts? And why did she have to be late? Twenty minutes, so far. But then, somehow, he knew that she always ran just a little behind schedule. She would forget something and go back for it and then decide she'd forgotten something else—the lights, the oven, her head.

He checked his watch one more time. He had the boarding passes in his hand. The photographer was here; Matt had fed him a lame excuse for Mo's not being with him, something about a last goodbye to her family. She wouldn't do this to him, would she? Not show up?

And then she was there, running toward him, her huge purse knocking against her. He offered a silent prayer of thanks.

Mo wore some sort of filmy, flowery long dress; flopping about her face was a large hat, which she held tight to her head with one hand as she made her way through the crowd that milled around. As she lifted that hand to wave to him, her purse dropped to the floor with a clunk, spilling some of its contents on the floor.

Mo skidded to a stop, bent down to retrieve her purse, and her hat fell off her head. A man in a brightly colored native robe tripped over her, but managed to retain his balance. Apologizing, he helped her load everything back into her purse, then assisted her in standing up, and was rewarded with one of her sunshine smiles. Grabbing her bag in one hand and her hat in the other, she came hurrying up to Matt.

"Hi," she said, out of breath, her cheeks rosy, her large blue eyes alight with excitement. "Sorry. I tried to get here on time, but there was a hassle with the key— my friend Laura is going to house-sit and I had to show her how to hold the snake and then she got kind of weird about it, but it's all right. And I'd forgotten to buy kitty litter."

"You have a cat, too?"

"No, it died. But the parrot likes kitty litter on the bottom of her cage instead of newspapers. And then there was the cleaners, the only nice dress I own, they had to rush it because I had to bring it with me. I mean, I figured I should have one nice dress with me, don't you think, even though it's old? Plus, I put my passport in a really special, secret place," she went rattling on, "but I forgot where and then I found it, guess where?"

"Where?"

"It was in the freezer! That way, if there's a fire, it's safe. The trouble was, some grape juice had spilled on it and it was pretty sticky so I had to wash it off. Then I put it in the microwave but I got scared it would burn so I finished the job with my hair dryer. I looked everywhere for that thing, even under the fish tank. Not the hair dryer, the passport.''

"Do you live in a zoo, by any chance?"

She laughed, then bit down on her bottom lip with small, white teeth.

"This her, Mr. Vining?" the photographer interrupted from behind him.

"Yes," Matt answered, snapped back to the practical world. "We just have time. Where do you want us?" he asked, turning toward the man.

The photographer, cynical-looking and middle-aged, with an unlit cigarette dangling from one side of his mouth, began taking shots even as he indicated the large Arrivals and Departures monitors against one wall. "Stand there," he said, clicking away, "with your arm around the bride. Better dump the purse, Mrs. Vining. And maybe the hat, too."

"Mrs. Vining?" Mo said. "Oh, that's me." She laughed again, more of a nervous giggle, and took her place next to Matt, stowing her purse and hat on the floor behind her. "Don't worry," she said, fluffing her gold-red curls. "I have a smaller bag inside this one. And comfortable shoes, too, like you told me."

"Good," he said.

Matt was a man to whom conversation came fairly easily; he liked words and knew how to use them. But Mo had this strange effect on him. With her, he found himself reduced to stunned, one- and two-syllable responses.

Could he have found anyone more wildly different from Kay? he wondered. No, probably not. Closing his eyes, he prayed silently, asking for strength to endure all the chatter, the noise, the *chaos* that seemed to follow Mo wherever she went.

The photographer positioned them, fiddled with his lenses and snapped some more pictures. Matt put his arm around Mo's slender shoulders, but lightly, impersonally. He had to keep this in perspective, he told himself, even as his nostrils detected her powdery, light flower fragrance, mixed with something lemony. It was an amazingly pleasant smell, earthy and otherworldly at the same time, and he breathed deeply, finding himself relaxing just a bit.

"You could hug her a little tighter," the photographer said, "maybe pull her to you. Didn't you two just get married?"

Married. Matt heard the word and remembered.

"Here, put this on," he said to Mo, reaching into his pocket and withdrawing a plain ring. "It had to be adjusted for size," he explained for the photographer's sake.

Mo didn't understand at first, but when Matt slipped the ring on the third finger of her left hand, she got it immediately. She stared at the thin gold band, amazed at how strange it felt to be wearing a wedding band. The ring was loose, but only slightly.

She glanced up at Matt at the same moment he looked down at her; their gazes locked, and she caught her breath. Oh, he had to have the most *soulful* eyes she'd ever seen on any living thing that wasn't a dog or a horse. A person could drown in those warm chocolate eyes, she thought, gladly, gratefully drown and not regret it.

"Thank you," she whispered, swept up with emotion. "It's a very nice ring."

"It goes along with the title of Mrs., I think," he said dryly. "And so does a look of bliss."

She grinned at him. He grinned back. *Click, click, click* went the camera.

"Good one," said the photographer. "How about a kiss?"

Mo watched as Matt bent toward her ever so slightly. But something stopped him. He remembered—she could see the thought take shape in his brain and reflect in his expression—that the two of them had an agreement, one she'd insisted on. There was to be nothing physical between them. Pretend only.

It would be difficult to pretend to kiss.

"How's this?" Matt pulled her closer so that her head was nestled in the crook of his arm, her cheek resting against his chest. He wore a lightweight sports coat, and its fine wool was soft against her skin. She heard his heartbeat, steady but on the rapid side. Like hers, she imagined. Closing her eyes, she cuddled up even more. So the picture would look authentic.

"Yeah, another good one." With several more clicks and a whirring sound, it was done.

Matt released her so abruptly she almost lost her balance. "I'm afraid that's all we have time for," he told the photographer. "We have some paperwork to take care of. Thanks."

Any intimacy between them—real or imagined—was broken off the instant he let her go. Mo shook her head to clear it. What had she been doing? Playacting, for sure, but then? Indulging in fantasy. For a change. Well, that would have to stop. She would rein in her wayward imagination, especially as Matt was back to his former self now—efficient, removed and all business.

Fine, she thought. In fact, good. It was time to get this show on the road. Ten thousand miles away, the silver-eyed man awaited!

* * *

When they were finally aboard the plane, in the air, ensconced in the plump luxury of first-class seats, Matt felt a little more inner tension slip away. They were here, they were on their way. It was real. He allowed himself a silent "Hallelujah!"

A loud sigh from Mo drew his attention to her just as she leaned back and closed her eyes. "Tired?" he asked.

"Really pooped. I haven't slept since yesterday. You?"

"Not a wink."

Her eyes snapped open and she turned to face him. "You had all that wedding stuff to deal with. What did you do? I mean, what did you tell people?" She grimaced self-consciously. "I'm sorry. It's none of my business, I know, so you can tell me to shut up—"

"It's all right," he said. "Kay, my ex-fiancée, took care of it all. She's very efficient. And it wasn't going to be a large wedding. Just a few friends and family."

"Still…" She paused meaningfully. "This must be a difficult day for you."

Matt considered how to respond to that. He wasn't really sure just what kind of repercussions his aborted wedding was having. In all the rush, he'd barely thought about it. The truth was, he'd barely thought about Kay— which probably didn't speak well for the depth of his feelings for her. So why *had* he asked her to marry him?

His career was going well. In the three years of its existence, the radio show had built a nice following in San Francisco, not an easy town to break in as a food expert, there being a glut of the species already. He wrote regular columns for some midsize newspapers. A hired public relations firm had been pushing his name, there was the book and a cable TV contract in the works. He was getting there, but he wanted more.

All his life, he'd been driven, first to turn himself into someone to respect, then to get an education, then to make a name, to be known, to be someone. But focusing on those things so much had taken a toll. Recently, he'd found himself missing something that had no name. That was why he'd wanted to marry; he'd thought Kay would slide into his life without a ripple and alleviate the loneliness.

That *did* sound pathetic.

Not only did he not care for that particular insight, Matt didn't think he really wanted to trade intimacies with Mo. Still, she deserved some sort of response to the tentative feeler she'd put out about his state of mind.

"Yes, the day has been difficult," he said evenly, "but, if you don't mind, I'd rather not talk about it."

"Of course." She was all compassion and understanding. "But I'm here, Matt, I want you to know that. I know I talk a lot—"

He felt the corner of his mouth quirk up. "I hadn't noticed."

"But, believe it or not, I also know how to listen. Everyone tells me all kinds of stuff. You can too."

What a sweet smile she had. He found her declaration comforting. Touching, really. "Thank you."

Just then, a yawn seemed to take Mo by surprise and she covered her mouth as she yawned again. "Sorry. I'm really beat."

"Can you sleep on a plane?" he asked her.

"I'm not sure. I haven't flown a lot—and then only on short hops. How long will this take?"

"Ten hours. And when we get there, it'll be noon tomorrow."

"Noon. In London." She crossed her hands over her heart. "Oh, gosh, I really can't believe this is happening to me."

Her enthusiasm made Matt's mood lighten even more. Maybe it wasn't such a crazy thing he'd done, after all.

The flight attendant offered them pillows, blankets, fancy nuts and drinks. Feeling like a kid in a free toy store, Mo took two of everything and turned to Matt, laughter bubbling up inside. "So, this is first class. I like it. It's just like on the commercials. You're probably used to it, huh."

Matt closed his eyes. "Hmm."

He really did look exhausted, she thought. There were shadows under his eyes. She hadn't noticed them earlier, she'd been so self-absorbed with her new adventure. Poor man. This was to have been his wedding day. He must be so sad, and covering it up so well. He'd made it clear he wouldn't discuss it. That's how it was with some people. Not her, of course. Mo liked to get everything out in the open as soon as possible, so it didn't fester and explode later.

She studied Matt's profile as he lay with eyes closed. Short thick black lashes shadowed his cheek. His nose had that bump that was quite appealing. And she had the most insane urge to run her fingertips over his cheek where the hint of a new growth of black beard appeared just beneath his olive skin.

Another of those nervous giggles rose in the back of her throat. She was so tired, yet so keyed up, she was practically on the edge of hysteria. She needed to splash some cool water on her cheeks.

"I'll be right back," she whispered, rose from her seat and went into the lavatory.

After she locked the door behind her, she scrubbed

her face and rinsed out her mouth. Then she stared into the mirror; there were shadows under her eyes, too, but there was a glow about her that even she could see.

"Thank you, *Nagyanya*," she whispered, and as she did, memories came pouring back. Soft, wrinkled, old skin. The smell of glycerin and rosewater hand cream, and the lime Life Savers her grandmother had loved so. Small bright eyes, large bosom and large arms, great for hugging.

Nagyanya had been one of the only people in the whole family that could get Mo to sit still, but always gently, with patience and love. During Mo's childhood, the old woman's stories, half English, half Hungarian, had held her enthralled for hours.

In the mirror, Mo watched her reflection as she flattened her palms against her flushed cheeks. *Nagyanya* had taught her to dream. But this wasn't a dream. She was here and it was real.

So was the attraction she felt toward Matt, the one that had started yesterday. It had gotten a grip on her libido and her head, and hadn't let up in the least. Through all the running and calls and planning last evening and this morning, she'd had Matt Vining with her the whole time, like an inner-ear hum that wouldn't go away.

But why? Mo was supposed to be with someone else—a man with silver eyes. She simply couldn't dismiss her grandmother's prediction. To ignore the sheer *coincidence* of how she had gotten on this plane and where she was heading, well, that would be the height of arrogance, wouldn't it?

So, Mo figured the silver-eyed man, not a brown-eyed food expert with a broken heart, was where her destiny lay. And she'd better keep that uppermost in her mind.

That thought, she wasn't really surprised to discover, caused a little twist of disappointment in the area of her heart.

When she returned to her seat, she found that Matt was not only wide-awake, but had chosen their dinner from several selections; he hoped she didn't mind.

"Fine with me," she said, helping herself to another handful of nuts. "I'm starving."

"You might want to save your appetite."

"My mother always used to say that. But I'm more of a nibbler. I pick a little all through the day." She shrugged and took some more nuts. Why did first-class snacks taste so much better than coach? A higher-grade nut? "It's how my system works, I guess."

A frown appeared between Matt's eyebrows. He disapproved of her eating habits, she supposed. Hmm. She shrugged mentally as she swallowed the last mouthful. Really, she was too tired to care. Her eyelids fluttered closed, and she nodded off.

Matt tried to sleep, too, but his five-minute catnap had taken the edge off. Instead, he read over some notes for his book, glancing occasionally at Mo. She slept, as she did everything else, with energy. She mumbled. She changed positions often. At one point, her head found its way to his shoulder and he let it stay there. Her hair smelled as though she washed it with springtime.

He woke her up as dinner was being served. She seemed groggy, and he told her food was just the thing to fix that. The flight attendant brought them each a glass of chilled white wine—quite decent, really—which Matt sipped appreciatively and Mo declined.

"I'm not much of a drinker," she said. "Just Coke and the occasional beer."

The appetizer was stuffed mushrooms with an interesting hint of sage. More than decent, Matt thought, rolling a forkful around in his mouth. Especially for airline food.

Mo took a bite, looked at it as though she'd just tasted castor oil and put the mushroom back on the plate.

"I guess I'm not very hungry," she said.

"Too many nuts?"

"Maybe. And I'm not a big mushroom fan. Something about the color. Also they're so…slimy."

"Wait till you taste truffles. You'll change your mind." It might be fun, he thought, to introduce her untutored taste buds to new food textures.

When the main course was served, Mo took a forkful, frowned and put down her utensil. "Oh. This is fish."

"That's what *poisson gribiche* is."

"I don't care for fish. Never have."

Mo couldn't help noticing that the frown between Matt's eyes grew more pronounced when she declared her aversion to slithery things that lived in the water. Yes, she had specific food likes and dislikes, but didn't everyone? He was simply hitting on a lot of dislikes at one meal.

"Perhaps," Matt said with a hint of arrogance, "you've never had fish cooked properly."

"Mom used to roll it in bread crumbs and fry it and pour ketchup all over it to get me to eat it, but fish is fish."

"Have you had it in *sauce matelote?* Cayenne pepper and wine? Or scallops *mousseline*, made with hollandaise and whipping cream?" He smiled mysteriously, his nostrils flaring slightly. "Have you ever sampled a lightly buttered fillet of sole so fresh it slides down your throat without chewing?"

Listening to Matt's rich baritone, watching his mouth

as he spoke was...well, it was downright sensual. "I still don't like fish, but I sure like the way you talk about it."

He seemed startled by her statement. "It's my field."

"It sure is. Listen, Matt, believe it or not, I like a lot of food, but—I confess—it's mostly junk food. I've always loved it, probably always will."

That frown again. "All those fats and chemicals. It's so bad for you."

Mo was definitely getting irritated. Matt's judgmental attitude was bringing out her combative side. She was the youngest of eight, and had learned to deal with authority by refusing to honor it. Mo was a doormat for no one.

"I can read health columns, too," she said with a touch of what her father used to call snippiness. "Hey, is this going to be a problem? I mean, you didn't mention that having the same food preferences as yours was a requirement for this trip."

"No, but I am going to be reviewing several four-star restaurants."

"Yes, *you* will be doing that. Does that mean *I* have to review them, too?"

Really, she thought, the man did have a streak of pomposity. She wouldn't stand for being treated as though she were some pesky schoolchild. No way she would put up with that for the next two weeks, and Matt needed to know it now.

"Well," she challenged. "Do I?"

One jet black eyebrow was raised, then he nodded slowly. "You're right and I apologize. Of course you don't have to share my taste buds, but—" now he nodded more confidently "—your entire palate will change on this trip, I promise you. You'll even learn to like fish, especially in Paris.''

"I wouldn't count on it.''

4

There were more photographs taken at the airport when they arrived in England, then a taxi ride from Heathrow through overindustrialized countryside. Eventually, they drove along a broad street filled with all kinds of famous sights, including Buckingham Palace, then to their hotel, a large stone edifice near Covent Garden. Humming "Wouldn't It Be Loverly?" all the way up the "lift," Mo followed the bellman into the suite—and oh, was it wonderful! Victorian, mostly, lots of antiques, Turkish carpets, painted flowers on the wallpaper and fresh ones in vases all around the room. An enormous fruit basket and champagne in an ice bucket sat on a side table, awaiting the newlyweds.

Mo whirled around the room, inspecting everything, the maroon-velvet settee, the spacious, lace-curtained windows with a view of the Thames, across which spanned Waterloo Bridge. Waterloo Bridge! The very name conjured up graceful women in Empire dresses, and ships appearing out of the fog, and men in full battle dress, wearing tricorn hats.

Sighing with contentment, Mo pushed open a pair of ornate double doors to the bedroom. It too was darling and fussy, made up of frills and flowers and lots more lace. It even had a four-poster bed hung with rich tapestries.

"Oh," she said. "Isn't this all too incredible?"

Matt, right behind her, scratched his head. As Mo inspected the "loo," he glanced at the double bed, then back at the small settee in the sitting room. How, he wondered, would he unfold his long legs on that?

Mo pirouetted back into the room. "I love it all! I'm going to change, then I'm heading right out to see the sights. Coming?"

"Actually, it would be better if you napped first." Matt went into the walk-in closet and unzipped his hanging bag so he could unpack. "I've done a lot of traveling, and I find if you sleep the minute you get off the plane, you're not bothered by the time change and jet lag."

"Sleep?" Mo appeared in the closet's doorway, her head cocked to one side. "When I just got here?"

"I recommend it, most strongly. Remember, I've done this a lot."

Mo shrugged. "Sorry, I'm too keyed up. But please, you do that—sleep yourself silly. I'm taking off."

Leaning against the doorway, Matt draped his arms over his chest and watched her as she tore through the luggage the bellman had set on a wooden chest at the foot of the bed. Her clothes seemed to have been packed with some semblance of order, but by the time she withdrew shoes, a pair of jeans and a striped cotton sweater from the bowels of the suitcase, its contents looked like the aftermath of a rummage sale.

She ran into the bathroom to change and he stared at the closed door, pondering.

Matt liked order. Maybe, he admitted, to a degree that was beyond reasonable.

Still, the way to get order, he'd found, was always to be in charge.

Obviously, no one was ever in charge of Mo.

"All right," he found himself saying to the closed door, "let's make this deal. I'll join you now if you agree to nap before dinner."

Mo poked her head out and said, "You don't have to."

"I want to."

"You got it."

"The dinner plans have changed, by the way," he told her. "Our reservations were for tomorrow night, but there's some royal fuss or something then, so it has to be tonight."

"Royal fuss?" She came out of the bathroom, tucking her sweater into her jeans.

"Some princess of something or other. They're taking over the entire Arbuthnot Restaurant."

"Oh, is that how it's pronounced? I think I read the name somewhere—an old Lord Peter mystery or something. Well, good, it'll be fun. Coming?"

She turned to the mirror over a finely carved chest of drawers and gathered her hair onto the top of her head, then did things with pins and clips so that it stayed up there. Matt was always fascinated by the way women did that, taking all that wildness and taming it. In Mo's case, of course, it was more a matter of keeping it at bay.

But he couldn't help noticing the way the movement of her arms pulled her sweater tight over her rib cage, so that he was treated to the sight of her small waist flaring out to shapely, jeans-clad hips and derriere. He was reminded, just for a moment, of a painting he'd seen as an adolescent of a woman in front of a mirror, pinning

up her hair, and the way his then-undisciplined, hor-
mone-driven body had reacted to the sight, right in the
middle of a museum.

"Matt?" Mo's eyes met his in the mirror. "Are you
okay?"

Shaking his head to clear it, he sternly ordered his
body to behave. "Just a little light-headed, I guess, from
traveling. I'll be ready in a couple of minutes."

As he headed off to change clothes, Mo said, "Tell
me something. Are we supposed to keep up this newlywed stuff for the whole trip?"

He paused in the dressing-room doorway. "What do
you mean?"

"You know, in the lobby, on the street... I mean, do
we have to hold hands and look into each other's eyes
and sigh? That kind of thing?"

Matt was aware that somewhere inside he was actually
disturbed—hurt?—by her question. Apparently, she
would prefer no physical contact with him at all. "I
would say not. Only if we're posing for pictures, or need
to seem married for the purposes of getting information
for the book. Okay with you?"

He kept his tone deliberately neutral, and when she
answered with a hearty, "Great," he frowned and
yanked at the zipper of his suitcase a bit harder than
necessary.

Mo was in heaven. Just walking down the street and
hearing all the various accents from passersby—high-
class, low-class, Pakistani, Jamaican. Just gazing at the
buildings, the old mixed with the new, the seedy and the
grand, the slums and the castles. All of it, sheer heaven.

Back in the States, Mo's two favorite pastimes were
watching travelogues on TV and browsing through the

travel sections of bookstores, so she knew quite a lot about what they were seeing. But actually to be here, in the flesh, well, it was past words.

As they exited their hotel Mo said, "I love to walk. It's the best way to really see a city, don't you think? So, today, I'd like to walk, and walk some more, until I pass out, hopefully near the hotel."

She could see Matt bite back a cautioning reply. Then he shrugged. "Okay, this is your call."

As Mo and Matt crossed the crowded piazza of Covent Garden, bustling with the summer's first tourists, she was an enthusiastic audience for the sidewalk entertainers—singers, musicians, jugglers, mime artists—who performed for passersby. She and Matt wound their way through a warren of boutiques and colorful street stalls and on into the Market Building—a huge, skylight-covered mall with lots of shops.

Several blocks north on Neal Street Mo exclaimed happily over the odd things for sale, everything from apricot tea, harmonicas and vintage bomber jackets, to halogen desk lamps, shoes with heels lower than toes and Afghan tribal jewelry. She picked out a few trinkets for various family members, paid for them with pounds and pence then shoved everything back into her oversize purse, which she had neglected to leave in the hotel room.

She and Matt walked, as she'd requested, then walked some more. They visited St. Paul's Church, known as the actors' church because of all the theaters in the parish, and strolled past The Strand to the Victoria Embankment Gardens—where the homeless and the tourists seemed to coexist—and stood at the edge of the Thames River.

"Cleopatra's Needle," Mo said, pointing to the sixty-foot pink granite obelisk ahead. She turned to Matt and beamed at him. "I've been hearing about this my whole life. *Nagyanya* told all of us about it. She came over from Hungary via London, and worked at the fruit markets in this area till she got on a ship to America. This was the one thing she remembered, above all. How this large, pink, kind of silly thing rises into the heavens."

He responded to Mo's story with that rare, unexpected smile of his, the one that turned his eyes warm in an instant.

There, she said silently. There's the real Matt, the one underneath his take-charge, autocratic exterior.

She liked him, she was amazed to realize. Funny, they had nothing in common and he could be kind of off-putting, but she liked him.

And as for that class-A body—well, she had to admit it, because she tried never to lie to herself, that the man was definitely sexy. In fact, Mo was still attracted to him big time.

But, sometimes she irritated him, it was obvious. And vice versa. The two of them were like male and female sandpaper, rubbing each other the wrong way. Which could be kind of interesting, as far as being attracted went.

No, she warned herself. *No.*

Even if the two of them got past their incompatibility, Matt had just been dumped by his fiancée, and there was no way Mo was going to be a rebound lover.

Even if he wanted her.

Which he didn't seem to.

Which was fine because Mo could hardly wait for her first glimpse of that silver-eyed man by the Danube.

Stifling a yawn, Matt watched as Mo tore the pins and clips out of her hair and tossed them onto the dresser.

"I think I'll hop in the shower," she said. "I feel really grungy. Unless you want to first?"

"No, I'll wait till after we nap." Matt picked up the phone and requested a wake-up call in two hours. He could hear the sound of running water from the bath, then Mo's voice singing something about steam or cream, he couldn't really make it out. He was past exhaustion and wondered where in hell the woman found all her energy.

According to his calculations, it had been forty-four hours without any significant sleep for either of them; he was feeling as though all the juices had been sucked out of him, and Mo was vocalizing like a diva about to make her debut at the Met.

He grabbed his briefcase and sat on an armchair so he could look over the itinerary. Instead, he set the paperwork aside, rubbed his eyes, then closed them.

And again heard Mo in the shower, now singing a mournful-sounding love song, and he pictured her soaping herself. He groaned. Amazing how easily he filled in the image from what little he knew.

That outfit the first day had given him a view of her legs, and everything she'd worn since had impressed the outline of her body in his mind. The woman had an honest-to-God hourglass figure, voluptuous breasts, a perfectly indented waist, rounded hips and amazingly long legs for someone so short. A pinup fantasy, slightly in miniature.

He smiled. He would never utter that thought out loud. Mo didn't appear the type to find being compared to a centerfold a compliment. Of course, you could never tell with women; some would like it, some would not. They seemed to get upset over the oddest things.

He liked quiet, competent, conservatively dressed, *tall*

women. Mo was none of those adjectives, not one. So why did all these semi-pornographic pictures keep popping into his head?

Matt moved over to the settee and lay down. His head was at an awkward angle and his feet hung over the edge, but he was so tired, he would have found a cave floor acceptable. He closed his eyes and was just about to drift off, when he heard, "Sorry you have to sleep on that thing."

He raised heavy lids to see Mo standing in the doorway of the sitting room, a Japanese kimono wrapped around her as she towel-dried her newly washed thick curls. The expression on her face was sympathetic.

He shrugged. "I offered."

"Maybe you could call housekeeping and get a rollaway bed or something. Or sleep on the floor—that carpet is as thick as a lot of sleeping bags I've seen. Do you ever go camping?"

"Not for years. I'll manage."

"All right." Leaning against the door frame, she emitted a long sigh. "Gosh, it just hit. All my bones have turned to jelly."

"It's jet lag." He refrained from saying, I told you so. "You'll feel better later."

"I'm counting on it." Keeping a hip against the door frame, she went back to toweling her hair. "So, what kind of restaurant are we going to?"

"Indian. One of the best in the world, I hear. I'm looking forward to it."

"Curry and stuff, huh. I've never had Indian food."

Lowering his lids again, he smiled. "It's a little more than just curry."

"You're the expert. Well, sweet dreams."

"I've left a wake-up call."

"Good. I need about twenty minutes to get ready."

"If that's so," he said, opening one eye to look at her, "you're the first woman I've known that does."

She favored him with a huge grin. "Okay. Twenty-five."

She turned away from him and, continuing to rub her hair, gently closed the door that separated their rooms. What flashed into his mind was Mo tossing the towel aside and dropping her robe to the floor, offering him a fine, full view of her tapering back and firm, rounded buttocks.

"Great," Matt muttered, attempting to turn on his side. As fatigued as he was, he could actually feel his body stirring. *No*, he thought. *Cut that out.*

Still, as he drifted off to sleep, it crossed his mind to wonder if, just maybe, Mo would be interested in changing the terms of their agreement....

5

Dinner began well enough. The restaurant was decorated in softly draping curtains of bright colors, with brass-accented, intricately carved fixtures. Quiet sitar music joined the tinkling of bells and the smell of nutmeg, saffron, anise and other spices, to create a most authentic Indian atmosphere.

Mo looked enchanting in one of her flowing, filmy concoctions that was sheer without being revealing, that seemed free-floating but clung to the outline of her body as she walked on high-heeled sandals. The dress had been her mother's, she'd told him.

She wore her hair partly up and partly down, with lots of curling red-gold wisps framing her face. She wasn't wearing a bra, Matt observed, swallowing as he did, and very little makeup. She didn't need either.

As a food critic, Matt had informed her, he usually sampled a variety of dishes, so he quickly focused his attention on the menu's careful selection of delicacies, then made some notes in a small journal. Meanwhile, Mo loaded up on the *na'an* and *poori* bread—subtly flavored with garlic and black onion seeds—and chattered happily after each mouthful.

"I was reading about that little pub we passed, on Rose Street? The Lamb and Flag? It used to be called the Bucket of Blood.'' She shivered. ''Isn't that awful? I mean, who would want to have a drink at a place called the Bucket of Blood? It was named that because they held all these boxing matches there. Do you like boxing?''

''Actually, I do.''

''Really? So does my dad. I hate it.'' She took a bite of bread and chewed it. ''This is delicious.''

In between bites, she took a few sips of wine. One of her sleeves sank into a plate of cucumber, onion and tomato relish and she winced, then rubbed at the stain with water from her glass. When the mulligatawny soup was served, she put a spoonful to her mouth, declared it too spicy and dug into the bread again.

The main courses were a superb *padsheh z'affran murgh,* or saffron chicken, and an excellent *hyderbadi korma,* lamb curry with yogurt. Matt studied the composition of the food on the plate, closed his eyes and sniffed at the hot, spicy aromas rising in front of him and nodded. So far, so good. More than good. Excellent. He began to eat, slowly savoring each mouthful. Cilantro, cumin, a touch of cinnamon. Yes, definitely first-class.

He glanced over at Mo to see her staring at him, her mouth slightly open and a dazed look in her eyes. When she realized he was looking at her, her cheeks flushed and she dropped her gaze to her plate.

''Everything okay?'' he asked.

''Just fine.''

Matt went back to his dinner. He was already composing a sentence about the *tori ka dal,* a zucchini dish, when Mo sighed and pushed her plate away.

''Gosh, I'm just too full,'' she said.

"You can't be serious. Please, one taste. This Peshawari chickpeas is the best I've had, even in Bombay."

"You've been to Bombay?"

"Two years ago. Please try it."

She gathered a bit of food on the edge of her fork and put it gingerly into her mouth. Then she made a small face. "It's...not my kind of thing," she pronounced, putting the fork down. "Sorry."

Matt felt inordinately let down by her reaction, and it must have shown because she said anxiously, "What's wrong?"

"It's just that Kay and I— Never mind."

Mo put her hand over Matt's. His skin warmed under her gentle touch.

"I'm sorry," she said. "I've been insensitive. You must be missing Kay a lot."

He thought about that for a moment, then replied truthfully, "Actually, it's not that. It's just, well, we both enjoyed dining. Kay was, still is, of course, a master chef. It's her career."

"Oh, I see." Mo withdrew her hand and picked up another piece of bread. "You were colleagues, then."

"Yes. It was something we had in common."

The only thing, really, Matt amended silently. Still, he used to enjoy his and Kay's spirited discussions over dinner. Of course, there had been all those silences in between....

He preferred conversation to introspection. "So, tell me about your career."

"I told you. I don't have one, not really."

"Not even a wish?"

She shook her head. "I've always worked, since high school, but not at one thing. I've been, let me see—" she counted off on her fingers "—a waitress, camp counselor, cosmetics demonstrator, school-bus driver, restaurant hostess, berry picker, bagel maker, door-to-door knife sharpener's assistant. And in between, I work at temp agencies. My typing isn't the greatest, but I'm good on the phone.''

"Good Lord."

"Yeah, a pretty long list, huh? Oh, and I also go to school. I have two years of community college and a bunch of credits in whatever interests me, which would never add up to a degree unless they have a Bachelor of Dabbling.''

"But, don't you want to finish college?"

"Nope. Or, anyway, not yet. Lots of time."

That bothered him, although why, he wasn't quite sure. He broke off a piece of bread and chewed it absently.

"I wonder if this was a mistake."

Matt looked up at Mo. He'd been wool-gathering again. "Excuse me?"

"You and me, here, the whole thing."

"A mistake? I don't think so. It's more of an adjustment, I suppose. What brought that on?"

"Well, you're sort of in mourning, and I'm not the right kind of person for this whole food thing, and besides, well, you're— No, never mind."

"I'm what?"

She waved away his question. "No, I don't want to get into this."

"Don't want to get into what?" He set his fork down firmly. "I hate it when people don't finish sentences. Please, I insist."

She spread her hands. "The fact is, I'm kind of impetuous and emotional and you're kind of, well, daunting to be with, I guess. Not very relaxed. Except, of course, when you're—'' Again she stopped abruptly.

''Except when I'm what?''

''When you're eating,'' she said with an embarrassed laugh. ''That's why I was staring at you before. I mean, when you lift your fork, you close your eyes and go into slow motion. You practically swoon when you put food into your mouth. You roll it around in there, I can almost see you basking in every little bit as it hits your taste buds. It's like...''

She paused, then blushed a rosy pink.

''It's sensual?'' he said with a small smile.

''That would be the word, yes.''

''I learned a long time ago that the aim of eating is not to devour food, but to cherish it. They do say eating is one of the most sensual experiences there is.''

''Yeah, well, for whoever 'they' are, and for you, I guess it is.''

''It could be for you, too. I'm afraid all that bread dulled your appetite.''

Mo closed her eyes for a moment and seemed to be either counting or gathering her thoughts. Was she annoyed with him? he wondered. What had he said?

Opening her eyes, she propped her elbows on the table and glared at him. The sleeve that wasn't soiled drifted into a dish of sweet mango chutney.

''Uh, your dress,'' Matt said, pointing.

Mo looked down, grimaced and lifted the fabric out of the sauce. She swiped at it with a napkin. ''Honestly, you can't take me anywhere. Everything I own has some kind of stain on it. I'm hopeless.''

She was a whirlwind, moving here, prancing there, never still, never deliberate. He wouldn't be surprised if her entire wardrobe spoke of every meal she'd ever eaten, every place she'd visited.

She was also adorable, a word he didn't ever remember using in his life. But she was. Absolutely adorable. Also genuine, vibrant and eminently huggable.

He verbalized none of these thoughts because Mo was definitely irritated with him. "Have I offended you?"

She looked up from dabbing at her dress. "Not really. I was about to, well, set the record straight." She put the napkin back down. "In case you can't tell, I don't share the same interests you do. I mean, maybe some of them, but not this one. I don't have this same...*passion* you do about food. I guess I'm mostly indifferent to it. It fuels my body, and once in a while I get a sugar craving or a need for something hot and greasy, so I go find a McDonald's or a Dunkin' Donuts, and indulge myself."

He shuddered. "How can you?"

"You're intolerant, you know that?"

"You're angry."

"More like aggravated. I don't really want to sit here and apologize for the way I am. I mean, am I going to have to spend the rest of the trip doing that?"

He studied her with a frown. "I didn't mean to give that impression, Mo. It's just that I so love what I do, I guess I'm having a hard time believing anyone can be indifferent to food."

Mo took another few moments to ponder just how to respond. Patience was required here, to get her point across, and patience wasn't her strong suit. "Okay," she said finally. "Do you like rap music?"

"Not particularly. But then, I don't know very much about it."

"Well, what would you say if I told you I have a hard time believing anyone can be indifferent to rap music?"

"Are you really comparing them? Fine food and—" he gestured vaguely "—street songs?"

"They're both sensual experiences, aren't they? There are creative, interesting rap songs and stuff that's just so-so. Like food. But both food and music appeal to the senses. One's taste, and the other's hearing."

"I suppose so."

"So, what if I asked you to go to a rap concert with me? And not just go, but really enjoy it? In fact, insist that you *love* it."

He looked at her with disbelief. "Rap music?"

"Hey, it's an interest of mine, sometimes even a passion. What's the matter, are you a snob?"

"I don't know. Am I?"

"Sounds kind of like it." Pausing, she grinned sheepishly. "I'm sorry. I'm being too hard on you."

He shook his head at her apology; from the furrow between his eyebrows, it was obvious that he was considering what she'd said. Then that face-shifting smile of his altered his expression from distanced to accessible. It's effect was like warm brandy on a frosty night.

"You're not the first person who's called me on that, you know." He nodded slowly. "All right, I'll try to be less intolerant. The next time I get on my high horse, feel free to let me know."

She stared at him. "Really?"

"Yes."

All her annoyance with him dissolved in an instant. "Wow, that's really terrific of you."

He chuckled. "I'm glad you find something about me terrific."

"Oh, I do. In fact, I—" Mo bit her lip before she

could wax eloquent on just how terrific she found him. Nope. That was one sentence that would remain unfinished.

"In fact," she said instead, "well, I'm having a wonderful time."

"Good. Now, here's what I suggest. I'll try to lighten up about the food, if you promise not to take me to a rap concert. Deal?"

"Deal."

"And I really can't talk you into one bite of this *kofta?*"

"The truth is, the smell reminds me of something that I don't think I'll mention, not at the dinner table. My stomach is shuddering at the thought. I guess Indian food is all a little too exotic for my tastes."

They finished the rest of the meal companionably. Mo even had a taste of the *kheer,* declaring it kind of like rice pudding. When he told her it was rice pudding, she wrinkled her nose and laughed. "So, why don't they call it that?"

Afterward, they decided to take a stroll and talk some more. The evening was pleasant and cool. It had rained briefly while they'd been inside the restaurant, and they walked along the slick, shiny streets of Soho, along Shaftsbury Avenue, with its many theaters and cinemas.

Mo told Matt about her family—her mom and dad, who ran a corner convenience store, her seven brothers, five sisters-in-law, all her nephews and nieces. She told him how great it was to have a large, loving family— and how awful it was to have a large, loving family.

"We have a hot line. Something happens to one, everyone else knows about it within ten minutes. A divorce, losing a job, a hangnail, everyone knows everything. Before I came on this trip, I had about forty phone calls, lots of advice, clucking, travel tips, warnings about taking along toilet paper. I mean, you would have thought I was going into space.'' She sighed. ''I love them to death, but sometimes I'd like to snap my fingers and make them all go away.''

Matt shook his head. ''I have no idea what that's like. None.''

''Were you an only child?''

''Most of the time.''

''Excuse me?''

''My mother had a hobby called marriage,'' he said sardonically. ''She did it on six separate occasions. We moved a lot. Sometimes I had stepbrothers and -sisters, but never for long.''

Mo didn't answer for a little bit. ''That must have been tough,'' she said finally.

''It was interesting, for sure. We got to travel a lot. I've lived in three different countries, and by the end of the sixth grade, I'd been to seven different schools.''

''You may call it interesting, but I call it a difficult way to grow up.''

It had been difficult, often painful. But Matt was unused to talking much about his past, even though, as she'd said, Mo knew how to listen. Still, something squirmed inside; he hadn't opened up the Pandora's box of his childhood in a long time. And he was reluctant to do so now. It seemed...needy, somehow.

He changed the subject. ''Are you tired yet?''

''You bet.''

''After a good night's sleep, we'll be back to normal by tomorrow. Why don't we head to the hotel? I need to make some phone calls to the States and scribble some notes for the book. I want to record my impressions of the meal while it's fresh in my mind."

"Oh," she said. "Well, then, I guess I'll see you later. I'm going to check out the city at night."

"We can go anywhere you want tomorrow. Besides, you can't travel around London alone after dark. It can be quite dangerous."

"Sorry. I really want to see the Thames by moonlight." She whirled around with her arms up in the air. "I've always loved water, especially rivers, which is one of the reasons *Nagyanya* made her prediction about the Danube. Maybe in another life, I was a water sprite."

She whirled away again. Matt caught up to her and put his hands on her shoulders to make her stop.

"Water sprite? Listen, you simply cannot do this. You cannot go traipsing about alone in a strange city at night."

"Excuse me, but I *can* do that. I *will* be doing that. Right now, as a matter of fact."

And with that, she marched off down the street, determination in her every stride. Matt watched her go, watched her hail a cab and get into it. He forced himself to stay where he was. No way was he going to run after her. No way.

A soft knocking made Matt rise, throw on his robe and make his way to the door of the suite. It was Mo, looking sleepy and apologetic. "Sorry," she whispered, "I forgot to take my key and I didn't know if I should ask the man at the front desk for another because we're supposed to be newlyweds and how would it look?"

He scratched his head and yawned. "It's all right," he said, stepping aside and letting Mo walk into the room. He closed the door and watched her walk toward the bedroom.

"I was in this little pub," she said, still talking softly in deference to the lateness of the hour. "It'll be good for your book. They have a thing called a newlywed corner, and everyone who passes by toasts them and buys them drinks. There's white ribbons and stuff all over it. Kind of corny, but cute. See you in the morning."

She floated into the bedroom and closed the door behind her. Matt lay back down on the settee and closed his eyes. A few moments later, he heard a soft knocking again.

"Matt?"

"Hmm?"

He opened his eyes to see Mo standing in the living-room doorway. She wore that silky kimono again, the one that silhouetted her luscious shape. His body responded immediately, as though it were on automatic pilot. He groaned silently at how she affected him.

"Thank you," she said softly.

"For what?"

"For the best day I've ever had in my life."

She looked down for a moment, then up at him again. He couldn't really see those large eyes of hers, but he had the feeling they were slightly moist, which wasn't really a surprise.

"And I owe you an apology," she said. "You were right. I shouldn't have gone off by myself like that."

Alarmed, he sat up, rubbing his hand over his face. "What happened? Are you okay?"

"Yes, I'm fine. I danced a little and had some of that awful warm ale, and then I slipped on some water on the floor—I'm always doing that—and there was this guy who caught me. He was pretty pushy. Kind of a biker type. He came on kind of hard, and I said no, very firmly, but he didn't want to hear it. I even showed him my ring—" she held up her hand, the gold band glinted in the moonlight "—but he didn't seem to care. Finally, this other guy with this wonderful cockney accent, Mick, his name was, came to my rescue. They didn't get physical or anything, but they did have some words. I think I learned how to curse in cockney."

Matt wanted to know what cockney cursing sounded like, but Mo kept up her usual river of words.

"It turned out that Mick was a cabdriver and he drove me back here. I was out of English money, but he took dollars. He was really nice. He has eight kids and one of them is named Maureen, like me... So, I'm okay. Anyhow," she said with a yawn, "like I said, you were right. I won't go out at night without you again."

She turned and went back into her room, shutting the door behind her. Feeling as though he'd just witnessed a film scene played at warp speed, Matt stared at the closed doors for a moment longer before trying to curl onto his side without too much of his rear hanging over the edge of the couch. Tomorrow, he would definitely ask for a cot, make up some kind of excuse—work, illness, whatever.

He was beyond tired; he was blithering with weariness. While Mo was out, he had not closed his eyes once because of worry over her safety; now that she was back, he was relieved, but most certainly not relaxed. He was puzzled by his reaction to her. He was not by nature someone who worried about others...or obsessed about them, either. That would mean people, relationships, connection had become important to him. And he'd shut down that part of himself long ago.

He wished Mo wouldn't take up room in his head like this, wished she liked fine cuisine, wished she were less of a free spirit and...wished he weren't attracted to her.

But he was. Damn. Pure lust, for sure. What else could it be?

The question kept him awake for a while longer.

6

With the living arrangements as they were, it was difficult to forget that Mo was around. The two of them had separate sleeping quarters, but there was one closet and one bath and they kept bumping into each other. Matt nodded to her the following morning as Mo was exiting the bath and he was entering. The room was filled with steam mixed with Mo's own personal aroma—baby powder, was it? Lemon? It surrounded him. It sank into his pores, invaded his head and made him dizzy. Also set off his libido and his imagination to the extent that, forgoing his usual hot shower, he took a cold one instead.

They breakfasted in the hotel's stately, high-ceilinged dining room, Mo's usual bright, chipper self reflected in her choice of a cheerful red minidress with a ruffle around the V-neck. This drew attention—his, anyway— to her more than ample endowments.

Announcing that she was starving, Mo dug into a huge English breakfast of eggs, fried potatoes, scones and marmalade. She turned down the kippers, of course. Matt, still full from the previous evening's meal, made do with a piece of toast and a cup of coffee, while Mo ate and talked, took a bite and talked some more of their plans for the day, of the reading she'd done on this city and all the others, of conversations she'd had the previous evening in the pub.

Matt watched her, fascinated by all the activity. It wasn't that Mo was a messy eater, exactly, more that she used food the way she used her life—voraciously, quickly and with a definite lack of tidiness. He watched as she licked the butter off a scone, then extended the tip of her tongue to the corner of her mouth, to catch a dollop of marmalade. His body tightened with desire at the sight; he wanted to lick it off for her.

This was becoming absurd, Matt thought. He was reacting like some randy sailor on leave. At some point, soon, he would have to do something about this impossible state of affairs. Or non-affairs, he amended.

He got his chance later in the day, after a boat trip along the Thames and more sight-seeing, before a scheduled stop at Regent's Park. The early-summer roses were in bloom, beds and beds of them, and Mo was exclaiming over the glorious colors, the sweetly pungent, individual smell emitted by each bush, when a small, thin man wearing plaid pants and a slouch hat came up to them.

"Mr. Vining?" The man spoke in a high-pitched, Northern English voice. "Simon Starkey's the name. I'm the picture taker."

Matt shook the photographer's hand, then introduced him to Mo. "Darling, this is Simon," he told her, putting his arm around her shoulders in a friendly, just-married-and-still-possessive manner.

"Hi, Simon," she said.

"Shall we pose here?" Matt asked the photographer, pulling Mo closer, and stroking her flesh softly, savoring the smooth feel of her under the pads of his fingers. The skin of her bare upper arm was warm from the sunshine. "With the rosebushes as a backdrop?"

"Don't need to pose at all, guv. I'll just tag along and snap away."

"Oh, then can we go to the zoo?" Mo said excitedly. "The area where all the birds are? I saw a whole TV show on it."

"Good idea, Mrs. V."

Simon ran around them, his camera clicking away, as Mo and Matt made their way through the park to the London Zoo, a lovely, animal-friendly place where moats separated the onlookers from its residents' habitats. No bars and cages; Mo liked that. She also liked the feel of Matt's arm around her, and was in no particular hurry to ask him to remove it.

They passed various animal exhibits until they arrived at Snowdon's Aviary. Row upon row of mesh cages were filled with thousands of chattering tenants. They were able to actually enter one of the huge, oddly shaped structures, one that reached taller than the tallest tree. Bits of blue sky were visible through the netting and towering branches. Mo gazed up with amazement at the fluttering wings of all the brightly colored creatures.

"Wow," she said, laughing with sheer delight. "Birdland, for sure."

"Right-o," Simon said as he took another picture. "Now, how's about standing in front of that bush there, the one with all the yellow flowers?"

"Shall we, my lady?" Matt said, and Mo angled her head up at him, ready to say, Certainly, my lord, when the expression on his face froze her for the moment. She caught him focusing on her mouth, his dark eyes even darker with some deep emotion.

He wanted her. He was trying to mask the intensity,

making an attempt at being casual and charming—and most of all, in control—but he wanted her. Even though his facial movements were subtle, she was reminded suddenly of a stallion sizing up a broodmare.

Mo swallowed nervously as something deep and primitive inside her responded to him. She wasn't sure what to do next, especially as she could feel her cheeks heating up, more than just her cheeks, actually. "Uh, I think he wants us over there," she said finally.

Matt nodded and, still holding her to him, aimed them toward the bush. They turned to face the photographer and Mo smiled self-consciously at Simon, but could feel Matt eyeing her instead of gazing straight ahead. The air was most definitely sizzling, and not with bird chatter.

"How about a kiss?" suggested Simon, obviously unaware of the unspoken sensual tension beneath the surface. Mo swallowed again and slowly turned her head to meet Matt's gaze.

He almost stopped breathing, that was the effect the woman had on him. Here she was, fitting perfectly into the crook of his arm; Matt imagined there would be a good fit between them whatever the activity. Her eyes, huge and questioning, were a glorious blue. Her copper and gold hair flew wildly around her face in the soft summer breeze.

With his free hand, he reached down to push a strand of hair off her forehead. Then he brushed his fingertips over her forehead, her eyelids—so soft!—and her cheeks.

More. He wanted more.

He ran his thumb across her chin, then over that incredible bottom lip of hers. He actually did stop breathing then, with the sheer pleasure of touching her.

"What...what are you doing?" Mo whispered.

"You still have a little marmalade there."

"Do I?"

He bent over and licked the corner of her mouth. "That's better."

"Oh." The word came out in a sigh.

Good God! Matt thought with shock, what was he doing? *Licking* a woman in public, in the middle of a zoo, in the middle of London, in the middle of the day!

Yes, as a matter of fact, that was exactly what he was doing. And what's more, he didn't give a damn who saw it.

Now his fingertips traced down the line of her neck, across her collarbone, and around the fringe of ruffles on her dress, barely touching the gentle swell of her cleavage and the dip between her two perfect breasts.

"Do I have marmalade there, too?"

"Unfortunately, no."

Part of his brain wondered why Mo wasn't protesting, but he wasn't going to bring it up. Birds swooped and chirped overhead, and somewhere nearby a child laughed. Matt had to kiss her. Had to. Propriety be damned.

Her mouth was trembling as he did; or was it his? Her lips were full and gentle and oh so enticing. He almost sighed aloud when he felt her ease closer to him, as though she too wanted more. Yes, yes, he wanted to shout. This was what they both wanted.

But not here, in the middle of a zoo.

Breaking the kiss, Matt smiled down at her. Mo gazed back up at him through dazed, half-lidded eyes, her breath coming lightly and rapidly through her parted lips.

"Did you get your picture?" Matt's voice was hoarse as he spoke to the photographer.

"How 'bout one more?"

Thank you, God. "Gladly," he said.

This time he couldn't pull off gentle. He commandeered her mouth and her tongue like a warrior claiming newly conquered territory. And she returned his enthusiasm by opening to him with an intensity that matched his own. Tongues and lips dueled and tasted and stroked; the inside of her mouth tasted like moist fire.

Mo had no time to think, no time to say or do anything. She was being swept up in a whirlwind of delicious, dizzying sensations and wondered vaguely if she would faint from the excitement. She had no idea how long they clung to each other, but eventually she heard Simon say, "Hey, guv, best come up for air."

This intrusion into the magic was enough to snap Mo back to reality. What was she doing? What was she allowing to be done to her? Her body was tingling, humming, crying out for more of the magic of Matt's mouth. Lord, the man could kiss! And Lord, she'd responded to his kisses as though she'd been starving for them her whole life!

None too gently, she untangled her arms from their clinch and eased Matt away from her. "Uh, I think the picture taking is over." She was unable to meet his eyes.

Simon sauntered up to them, nodding and grinning. "I got a bunch of good ones." He touched the brim of his hat. "It's been a pleasure, Mr. and Mrs. V. Enjoy your honeymoon." He snickered. "Although, it's obvious you already are."

Both Mo and Matt watched him stroll away. Two chartreuse parrots squawked loudly at each other and hopped onto a higher branch.

"Well," Mo said brightly, gazing up and around, everywhere but at Matt. "This is quite a place, isn't it?"

Matt placed a hand on her shoulder. Just that slight touch made her nerve endings flutter. "Mo," he began. "We've started something—"

"No." She shook his hand off and forced herself to glance up at him. "Please, don't. I don't want to be a substitute for Kay."

He seemed genuinely surprised. "You're kidding."

"No, I—"

She never got to finish her sentence because at that moment a jet-black bird dive-bombed between them, causing Mo and Matt to step back from each other. Then the creature flew up toward a branch, changed direction, swooped down near Matt's head, rose again and...

"Oh dear," Mo said. She couldn't believe what the bird had just done to the entire front of Matt's shirt. Covering her mouth with her hand, Mo bit her lips together so the laughter bubbling up inside her wouldn't escape.

In the space of a few seconds, Matt's expression went from startled, to offended, and finally to really annoyed. He reached into a back pocket for a handkerchief, and swiped at his shoulder and chest. Then his gaze met Mo's; he narrowed his eyes, as though daring her not to laugh.

But she did, she couldn't help it. Peals and peals of laughter, even though she tried hard not to. Eventually, Matt's mouth twitched a little on one side, then the other, and soon he too was laughing, a wonderful, rich roar of a laugh. The first she'd ever heard from him.

They collapsed against each other for a moment, catching their breath. Then Matt said, "I think it's time to escape this place, before I receive another token of appreciation."

They made their way back toward Regent's Park in

what seemed to be companionable silence. After a moment, Matt said, "We haven't finished our conversation yet."

"Sure we have."

"Mo, please, allow me to assure you that you aren't— you couldn't be—a substitute for anyone, most especially not Kay."

"Hah. That's what they all say."

"They all say you're not a substitute for Kay?"

"No, no, you know what I mean. Men. When they want you, they assure you they're over their girlfriend or their wife, or whatever, and then you believe them, but all they really want is to get in your pants and then they break your heart."

"Has this happened to you a lot?"

"Once is enough, believe me."

She knew she sounded more emphatic than she felt; the truth was, she was scared. That little necking session back there in the aviary had really thrown her, tossed her into space, really. Matt's kisses had affected her like no other man's kisses ever had. Right now, it seemed pretty important that Mo discourage any further moves in that direction.

She stopped near an empty park bench and turned to face him, her arms crossed over her chest. "Listen, what is this, Monday?"

"Tuesday."

"Okay, Tuesday. Two days ago, you got unengaged—"

"Three days ago." Matt looked at the handkerchief he was still holding in his hand, scowled briefly and tossed it in a nearby garbage pail.

Mo bit back a grin. She needed to be serious now, but he looked so cute when his dignity was threatened.

"Okay," she said reasonably, sitting down on the bench and gazing up at him. "Three days ago, your wedding was called off and you were forced to ask a perfect stranger to go on your honeymoon with you. See? I was supposed to be Kay, but I'm not—"

"You can say that again." He sank onto the bench next to her.

"So, you're probably filled with all kinds of anger, not to mention resentment for being cheated out of, well, what usually happens on a honeymoon, you know what I mean. So, I'm not trying to sound like a shrink or anything, but I think you're just a little too close to the situation to be objective and to know if I'm a substitute or a fantasy or what I am."

"You are most definitely a fantasy," he said, draping his arm casually over the back of the bench, just near her shoulders.

"Seriously, if you take a minute to think about it, you'll agree with me."

"I am serious, and for once in my life, I don't want to think. I wonder—" his finger made circles on the sensitive skin of her arm, and she jumped at the contact "—if you'd be interested in renegotiating our agreement, the part about platonic only?"

She shivered with sensation, then shrugged his hand away. "Hey, come on."

"Is that how you feel about me? Platonic?" He lifted her hand to his cheek and rubbed it over his recently shaved skin. Her palm burned and she heard herself sigh. Those meltingly brown eyes of his drew her into their depths until she wondered wildly if he was some sort of sorcerer.

"Well, uh, I—"

"Are you really going to say," he went on in a voice

that would have pulled down the covers on any bed in the world, "that I'm the only one feeling this attraction between us?"

Mo tried never to lie, really she did. But how would it sound if she said, yes, she was attracted, that she'd barely thought of anything else since they'd left the States? If you were an upright, unhypocritical type of person, what could you do with an admission like that except act on it? And she wasn't ready for that. No, really, she wasn't. So she equivocated.

"Time out."

She removed her hand from his and studied her lap. Then she let her words out in a rush. "You're a good-looking man, and a really fine kisser, I mean really fine, but all I want from you is friendship."

A moment passed, then Matt said dryly, "You may have observed that friendship is not what I'm feeling at the moment."

She allowed her gaze to wander down his body; he wore neatly pressed jeans that day, and it was impossible not to notice his rather prominent arousal. It was also impossible not to notice the thrill that rushed through her veins at the sight.

Irritated with herself for her reaction, she rose from the bench and began walking again. "Men," she muttered.

Matt followed. "Excuse me?"

"I said, all you men are so—" she threw her hands in the air "—filled with testosterone."

He had the audacity to find that funny. Grinning, he challenged, "And women don't get lusty?"

"Well, sure we do, but..." She stopped in her tracks and faced him, hands on hips. She had to set boundaries, and now. "Listen, I have a great idea. How about I leave you?"

"Go back to the hotel?"

"No, leave England. I could take my ticket and just go on to Hungary, to the Danube. That's why I came on this trip, anyway, right? Remember? The silver-eyed man? That way, you can do research for your book without having me in your hair."

Her hand flew to her mouth. "Oh, no, I'm sorry. That's right, I can't do that—I agreed to be your wife, I mean, your pretend wife." She grabbed some of her hair and clutched it between two fists. "Oh! You have me so crazy I don't know what I'm saying. But this whole—" she threw her hands in the air again "—sex discussion has got to stop!"

Matt stiffened as Mo's words sent a deep shaft of disappointment through him. What was happening here? How had he allowed this woman to affect him this way? And he'd never behaved so outrageously in public before. Not to mention that he was practically *begging* Mo to go to bed with him, something he'd also never done in his life.

Matt didn't think of himself as a vain man, but, frankly, on those occasions when he evinced interest in a woman, he wasn't used to being turned down, especially when he sensed the lady was just as attracted to him as he was to her. Which this lady was, he knew, even if she kept taking contrary action.

But why was he surprised that Mo never did the expected thing? Or that she caused him to act completely out of character? Didn't he get it yet? This woman was totally, completely unique, one of a kind, unheard of by mankind up to this moment. And she was his traveling companion.

For better or for worse.

Looking off into the distance, Matt made himself take a moment to calm down and gather his pride. Also to allow his body to get back to being unclenched—all over. Enough of acting the besotted, love-crazed suitor. He didn't even believe in the emotion, so why give it any credence? Finally, he nodded, knowing what he had to do and almost welcoming the decision, even with the disappointment, not to mention discomfort, it would surely bring.

"You're not in my hair," he said. Then, more resolutely, "Mo, all I really want to do is write a great book, one that will further my reputation and career. It's all I've ever cared about, to be truthful. As for you and me, well, I'm a grown-up and can certainly control my libidinal impulses. You might even be right about me not being over Kay yet. Yes." He nodded firmly. "Friends. We'll be friends. You have my word. Shall we shake on it?"

After an initial look of wariness, Mo offered up a tentative smile. "You did it again," she said wonderingly.

"Did what again?"

"Heard me. You listened, you thought it over, and took it like a champ. That's a really, well, admirable quality, you know that?"

He returned her smile. "One you value in a friend?"

"Better believe it." She put her hand in his and shook it firmly. "Friends."

7

They took one of the ferries across the English Channel the next day, to Calais. Matt couldn't help smiling as he watched Mo leaning on the railing; she was like an excited child as she stood with her head thrown back and her eyes closed, letting the ocean's salt spray bathe her face. After a while, she opened her eyes again and grinned at him, wiping her damp skin with the sleeve of her oversize peasant blouse.

"Can I thank you again for this trip?" she said.

"Sure."

"*Merci*, which is one of three French words I know. But, tell me, isn't this the slow way to France? I mean there's the new Chunnel, and all. Why did you choose the old-fashioned route?"

"That was Kay. She said, on a honeymoon, people should take their time and always choose the most romantic way to travel."

"Oh."

Mo gave him a look of warm understanding then went back to studying the view, the wind blowing her hair all around her and the sun glinting on its red-gold strands, making them seem like thin wires of living copper.

Friends. He'd kept the word and the concept of

"hands off" uppermost in his mind since agreeing to it yesterday. It wasn't easy.

Seagulls swooped and cawed loudly overhead. Mo seemed fascinated by their movements. Everything interested her; all the pleasure she took from just being alive glowed on her face. Reluctantly, Matt made himself stop looking at her and gazed instead at the fluffy white clouds over the channel and the waves sent up by the boat. Ruthlessly, he shut down any admiration he might be feeling toward Mo's hair, or the way the wind pressed the fabric of her clothing against the outline of that provocative body of hers.

She wanted friendship? She'd get friendship. Paris, France, the world-renowned City of Love, was about to receive two pretend honeymooners, two could-be-but-unfortunately-not lovers, instead of the real thing.

Mo adored Paris. After checking into the hotel, a large, rambling building that used to be the chateau of some count or duke three hundred years before, she and Matt went out to engage in her favorite activity—walking.

They strolled along the broad boulevards, past park benches where men puffed on cigarettes and argued in that beautiful language of theirs, and couples kissed in corners. They walked through gardens and under bridges, smelling the dampness from the Seine and the subtle scent of flowering chestnut trees.

Eventually, Mo requested something sinfully sweet instead of lunch, so they stopped for pastries at one of the city's hundreds of little cafés. This one, with tiny, marble-topped tables tumbling onto the crowded sidewalk, was near the base of the massive Arc de Triomphe. She told Matt that he could order for her, but to remember that she didn't require anything too fancy, just something sweet and greasy. Like Winchell's apple fritters.

He smiled and, in perfect French, requested *Mille-feuilles aux fruits rouges,* which turned out to be layers of thin puff pastry and fresh raspberries and strawberries. For himself, he ordered sweet biscuits and a glass of wine.

Mo's salivary glands started working overtime from the moment the dessert was set on the table until she finished every creamy crumb of it. Then she sat back and sighed. "That was heaven. Much better than Winchell's. Is this considered an A-type place?"

Matt finished making a notation in his notebook. "On a scale of fair to excellent, it's very good."

"Only very good? You mean, something could taste even better than this? No way, Matt."

He favored her with that knowing little smile that she had come to think of as his I'm-the-expert grin, and which she now found kind of dear instead of off-putting.

"There is a *pâtisserie,*" he said, "in a tiny town in the south of France that, legend has it, was founded by angels. Their pastry is the lightest, their cream the freshest, their fruits and sorbets the closest thing to heaven I have ever tasted. That is where 'excellent' is."

Leaning an elbow on the table, Mo rested her cheek in her hand and gazed at him. He looked yummy today, for a change, in a rust-colored cotton sweater with the sleeves pushed up, and a pair of brown slacks and brown loafers. His arms were corded with muscle, though not overly so. The sweater was slightly scoop-necked, and dark chest curls were visible above the neckline. He was shaved and tanned and, with that slightly broken nose, unbearably attractive.

Even as she found parts of her body humming while

she studied him, she wondered idly how his clothes always stayed so neat. Except, of course, at the London Zoo, when the bird had used him for target practice. She smiled at the memory, but shared none of these musings with him.

Instead, she asked, "With all this eating you do, why aren't you fat?"

He shrugged. "Metabolism. Plus, I don't eat like this all the time, and I work out at a gym."

"Really? I don't see you in sweats, somehow." Little tiny shorts, maybe, she amended silently. And nothing else.

"Why don't you?"

"Why don't I what?"

"See me in sweats?"

It was her turn to shrug as she tried to mask her embarrassment over her sudden mental pictures. After finding a little more pastry on her fork, she said, "I don't know. You're such an aristocrat."

"Me?" He chuckled. "Not even close. My mother was an underage cocktail waitress when she met my father. Husbands two and four were more financially comfortable than the others, and I guess I learned a little about clothing and manners from them. But I went all through school on scholarships. And I worked construction jobs during the summers. Sorry," he said ruefully. "There's not an aristocrat on any branch of the family tree."

Mo's mouth dropped open. "Wow, I can't believe this. I had you pegged as old money. Yacht clubs and debutantes and stuff. So then, how'd you get into this whole food thing?"

Sitting back in his chair, he said thoughtfully, "My mother's husband number four—Henri Chartier—was

French. His family ran a little place in Cherbourg, four or five tables only, and he cooked only what he wanted each night. There were always lines around the block.''

The look on his face grew more introspective, even tender. ''I had some of the best times of my life in that kitchen. The smells, the warmth of the oven, the laughter, the scarred old wooden cutting board and the huge white sink. The absolute delight they took from feeding people. After a while, I knew it was something I would be involved with forever. Even when my mother went on to husband number five,'' he added sardonically.

Mo felt a small wrenching in her heart at this revealing bit of Matt's history. She wondered if he was even aware he'd found something in that kitchen he must have been missing all his life. Biting her lip, she fought down a sudden urge to cry for a little boy desperate for nurturing.

She played with her napkin for a few moments until the threat of tears was past. Then she said softly, ''I find this totally fascinating.''

''Do you?''

''And you're fascinating.''

''Am I?'' He seemed surprised but amused.

''Yes. You're so...different from the way you appear.''

''You're not.'' His grin was wry. ''You register everything you're feeling, right on your face. Just now, you were sad, although I don't know why.''

He hadn't a clue, had he? Mo thought. No wonder he seemed distant so much of the time; he was distanced from himself, most of all.

She waved away the moment with an embarrassed laugh. ''It was nothing, a passing thought. So—'' she quickly changed gears ''—I'm easily readable, huh?

Shoot. And I've always wanted to be mysterious. The fascinating woman in the corner that everyone wonders about—'' she arched one eyebrow dramatically ''—but no one really knows.''

He shook his head, chuckling. ''Sorry. You're about as subtle as a billboard.''

''How boring.''

''Never that. On the other hand...'' He paused, his expression more serious now. ''You are sweet. And kind.'' Seeming to choose his words carefully, he went on, ''And real. And...quite, quite lovely.''

This last sentence was spoken softly, and it made her shiver with pleasure. Looking down at her plate, Mo said, ''Thank you,'' in a voice that sounded a little wobbly, even to her, and traced the table's marble pattern with her finger.

After a while, Matt covered her hand with his and squeezed. ''Come,'' he said. ''The city awaits.''

They strolled along more of the stately, tree-lined Avenue des Champs-Elysées, a little over a mile to the Place de la Concorde, a large square filled with flower beds and trees.

In a small section of the Jardin de Tuileries, a lovely park nearby, a street puppet show made Mo laugh, especially when she looked at the rosy-cheeked children surrounding the makeshift stage, their eyes wide and trusting. It was so comfortable being with Matt this way, without all that sexual tension in the air.

In fact, Matt seemed almost lighthearted today, and certainly less guarded. She watched as he walked over to a flower seller, picked out a rose and, bowing, presented Mo with it. She curtsied back and they grinned at each other. She sure liked the way his face creased up when he was happy, and the way his dark eyes got lighter somehow, becoming almost a dark amber.

Yes, this friends thing was good, Mo thought. Really good. She was glad he'd thought it over and decided she was right—the two of them did not belong together as lovers. He was probably even feeling silly about how hard he'd come on to her the day before.

He had stopped touching her at the slightest provocation, and studying her when he thought she wasn't noticing. Good. Obviously, Matt was over whatever he'd thought he was feeling.

She was sure pleased he'd had a change of heart, pleased he'd heard her.

Really she was.

The restaurant setting was certainly a major winner, perched as it was on a hill just across from—Mo could hardly believe it!—the Eiffel Tower. The view was of twin sandstone pavilions, the Palais de Chaillot, Matt had told her, which had a series of descending gardens and pools all the way down to the river. It took your breath away, she thought. Like something out of a fairy tale.

As the night was clear and only slightly chilly, they ate on the outside flagstone terrace, at a lovely umbrella table. White-coated waiters moved around them in near silence, and from the other tables came the sound of murmured conversation and soft laughter, and the smell of garlic and French cigarettes.

London had been great, but they all spoke English there. Being in France was a real foreign feeling. Exotic. And terribly exciting.

Mo wanted to be a good sport, so she promised herself

that during dinner, she would try at least to taste everything Matt offered her.

They started with wine, and after it was poured, Matt spoke softly to the waiter in his perfect French. When Mo asked him to translate, he told her, with a sheepish grin, that he'd asked him to hold the bread till the food was served. She decided to respond to this none-too-subtle hint by laughing it off.

Reading from the parchment menu, Matt translated some of the first-course dishes for her, and she got to choose between sautéed duck liver and beans, warm potatoes with gelatinous pig's feet, fresh sardines marinated in thyme, jellied spider crab and eggplant caviar in tomato sauce. *Yippee*, she thought silently.

In all honesty, none of them sounded appetizing, but she went for the duck liver because there was no way he was getting her to eat fish and she hated purple vegetables. The wine was pretty good, though, and she had a couple of spoonfuls of the duck. The beans were a little too spicy.

Matt ordered fillets of fresh marinated mackerel on a bed of "rosemary-infused tomato coulis," whatever that was, grilled pigeon and a roast rack of lamb sliced tableside. Also another, different bottle of wine. It was a good thing he wasn't paying for all this, Mo thought, because this meal would cost your basic arm and leg.

Still, it was all quite elegant, and Mo was glad she'd worn her black minidress with the beaded straps; it was pretty old, but still serviceable. Also that she'd brought along a shawl, after Matt had absolutely insisted on it.

He was in a perfectly tailored charcoal-gray suit with a soft yellow shirt and a silver tie. She almost sighed out loud. The way the man carried himself, well, for sure there had been some aristocracy—maybe even royalty—

in his bloodline. Or maybe in a previous life, if you bought into that kind of thing. Whatever, he looked good enough to, well, eat.

However, she reminded herself, he wasn't on her particular food plan. She was reserved for the silver-eyed man. A wave of guilt swept over her; she'd practically forgotten him altogether. It was best to bring him to the forefront of her mind and shove Matt to the back, where he belonged.

Mo had the lamb, which was too pink and needed salt, and refused both the fish and most especially the bird. Cute little pigeons? No way. She had her bread, though, and it was really good. Somewhere halfway through the meal, when Matt stopped asking her to ''just taste,'' Mo breathed a sigh of relief. She'd tried, really she had.

The photographer showed up, and took all kinds of pictures of Mo and Matt laughing and holding hands and feeding each other bites of food at the table. Matt actually tried to sneak a forkful of fish into her mouth without her knowing, but she got a whiff and actually spit it out. After blushing profusely and apologizing to the waiter, she glared at Matt as she gulped down some water. Matt apologized, but soon both he and the French photographer were laughing and she joined them.

The nice part about the picture session was that this time they were able to avoid all that fuss with pretending to be passionate. Good, Mo thought, tamping down another, slightly disappointed voice that informed her that she had kind of *enjoyed* all that pretending to be passionate.

At one point, when the waiter leaned over and asked, in thickly accented English, if everything was okay, Mo smiled sweetly and said, *''Oui.''*

To Matt, however, she confessed that French cooking

just wasn't her thing, except, of course, for that warm, crusty bread. Heaven. Poor Matt shook his head in wonder, but seemed to accept it with good grace.

They'd begun the meal at twilight, and by the time dessert was served it was completely dark. There were clouds over the moon and only a sprinkling of visible stars. In the distance, light came from the palace and the Eiffel Tower; the flickering candles at the tables provided a soft glow closer in. It was quite romantic, Mo thought, and kind of a shame they had to waste it. Being that she and Matt were only friends.

Dessert was, of course, more than okay, although her favorite so far had been the pastry that afternoon. They had a chilled peach soup, which was not sweet enough for her, and a bitter chocolate sorbet topped with hazelnut cream sauce. Mo tasted both, but preferred the sorbet, only without the sauce.

"Whew, I'm full," she said when the dishes were taken away.

"We're not quite done."

"Isn't the end of a meal the dessert? Oh, you mean coffee."

"No," Matt said, smiling.

Just then the waiter brought a platter of cheeses and apple slices, with small, sharp silver knives and new plates. And of course, another bottle of wine.

"What kind of cheese is this?" Mo asked Matt warily.

"There are four different varieties of *bleu*."

"You mean, there's more than one kind of blue cheese?"

"Several."

"Huh. Well, whatever. I'll have some apple."

The slices were good, tart and sweet at the same time.

She chewed one final bite, swallowed, then sat back in her chair. "So. Is the meal done now?"

"Coffee with brandy, and then we're done."

"Silly *moi*. Of course. But I think I'll skip the brandy. And I want you to know that I'm in love with Paris...in spite of the food. You're being really patient tonight, putting up with my low-life taste."

Shaking his head, Matt laughed good-naturedly. "You certainly do have your likes and dislikes. But you gave it a try, and that's all anyone could expect." Raising his wineglass, he said, "To Paris...in spite of the food."

Mo could drink to that. She could drink to a lot of things, actually. Had, all evening, as a matter of fact, and was now definitely tipsy. The meal had lasted about four hours and they'd polished off quite a lot of wine. She raised her long-stemmed glass to Matt and considered what to say.

Here's to sexy men in dark suits.

Here's to men named Matthew who tempt her something awful, in spite of her resolve.

No, to both. Not cool, in the least. All right then, what? "Here's to post office boxes," she said finally, then giggled and took one more sip.

"To post office boxes. And...friendship."

She glanced up at him, but in her current inebriated state, couldn't tell if that pause was ironic or not. "Yes," she agreed. "Good ol' friendship."

"And, my good ol' friend, I think we'd better get you back to the hotel."

A half hour later, as she and Matt stood side by side in the elevator, Mo noticed a couple of exquisitely dressed women giving Matt an appraising glance. Then one whispered slyly in the ear of the other, both of them laughing softly afterward.

Matt turned that slow, sexy smile on the two women, and Mo felt red-hot jealousy rise up and bite her. She wanted to shout at them, to raise her hand so they could see her ring, then maybe even raise a different finger to them. Hands off, she wanted to say. He was hers.

But of course, he wasn't.

She was being irrational; she knew that. Probably the wine. She'd had her chance and she'd said no. If Matt wanted to flirt with other women, maybe even to do more than flirt, well, it was nothing to her. Nothing.

The elevator opened at their floor, and Mo scowled surreptitiously at both women as she and Matt stepped out onto the thickly carpeted hallway. On their way to their room, Mo tripped once and Matt caught her around the waist. "Careful."

"Shoes wobbly," she said.

"Too much wine."

"That too."

"Are you going to be all right?"

"Sure."

The honeymoon suite had two separate entrances, one to the living room and one to the bedroom. Matt paused outside the latter. He used his key to open Mo's door and gently pushed her inside.

"Sleep well," he said.

"Where're you going?"

"I think I'll have a nightcap in the bar. I'd ask you to join me, but it seems to me you need your sleep more."

Are you going to meet someone there? she almost blurted out, but managed to bite her bottom lip before the words could escape. Obviously, he didn't want her with him. He wanted to put the moves on one of those simpering French "ladies" from the elevator. They'd probably passed notes and room keys to each other when Mo wasn't looking. She envied all French women, with their Chanel suits and their subtle perfume and the way they growled in the back of their throats when they spoke their language.

"Good night, Mo," Matt said. "Tomorrow we'll go to the islands right in the middle of the city. You'll enjoy it." He smiled again and closed the door.

She plopped herself down on the bed and frowned, assessing her condition. A little light-headed, she decided, but not sick. From the wine, anyway. The green-eyed monster was another thing, though.

A long, cool glass of water helped. Also washing her face and brushing her teeth, after which she crawled into the deliciously soft-yet-firm bed and pulled the down comforter over her. Faint accordion music from somewhere reached her ears. She stared at the ceiling, all carved curlicues and fat cherubs, while shadows from the lighted terrace made strange shifting patterns.

Somehow, as she remembered thinking back at the restaurant, it seemed such a shame not to take advantage of this romantic French atmosphere. Yes, a definite shame to waste a bed like this, a suite like this, a night like this, sleeping alone.

Hmm. If she wanted to, Mo thought, she could crawl into Matt's bed and surprise him when he returned to his room....

No, no. No! She'd worked too hard to establish this friend thing. Besides, he didn't want her with him anymore that evening. She could take a hint as well as the next person.

She wondered if Matt would be sleeping alone that night. The idea brought a sudden painful lump to her throat, but she knew if she thought about that, she might get really crazy. The inside of her head was whirling now, so she closed her eyes. After a while, she slept.

And dreamed of pastries and angels and men with eyes that went from silver to brown and back to silver again.

8

───── ◆ ─────

"I look awful," Mo said the next morning, removing large sunglasses and squinting as she sat down across from Matt. "I know it."

Matt had chosen the hotel's outdoor patio for breakfast. He had been waiting for Mo, at a table shaded by lime trees, for the past hour. "Not awful," he said, pushing a large cup of hot black coffee toward her, "just a little less cheerful than usual. Most people who drank as much as you did last night would look a lot worse the next day, believe me."

"Is that supposed to make me feel better?" Leaning her forehead on her hand, she shoveled several spoonfuls of sugar into her cup and stirred. "Besides," she said, after raising her cup to her mouth and taking a sip, "you drank as much as I did."

"The family hollow leg—we're famous for it. Also, with all the wining and dining I do, I've had to learn to pace myself."

"Well, I haven't. Right now, I don't care if I ever see another glass of anything vaguely alcoholic again."

"But you look so cute when you're hungover," he said with a laugh. She did, too. Her hair was pulled back in a high ponytail. There were still sleep lines across her cheeks and her eyelids were morning-heavy and without a trace of makeup.

Mo scowled. "I hate being called cute. And I wish I were five foot ten."

"Sorry." Matt bit back another smile. On this trip he'd seen her in various emotional states—warm, moved, irritated, joyful, turned on and flustered—but this was the first time he'd seen her grouchy. He found her in this mood, as he did in all of them, utterly adorable. He would continue to keep that thought to himself, however. If she hated "cute," "adorable" would make her come after him with a knife.

Drawing the cover off a silver tray, he said, "*Voila!* Croissants. Strawberry jam. Great for what ails you. They'll fix you right up."

"Plying me with bread again, are you?" She reached for one of the flaky crescent rolls and smeared jam all over the top.

"It seems to work."

After a few bites, some of the grumpy tension seemed to go out of Mo's body. With a contented sigh, she said, "I feel better already. I think there is definitely a God. And, when I taste a croissant, I believe his first language was French."

Resilient soul that she was, the food and coffee made Mo snap right to, and in short order, Matt and she were walking along the tree-lined quays of the Seine. The day was warm, the sky blue, and the streets filled with all the scenes of daily life in Paris: men in green uniforms sweeping excess water into the sewers with twig brooms; distracted drivers careening around narrow corners. Chess players, lovers. Matt saw and enjoyed all of this, as though for the first time.

"You know what?" he said, his heart light with an emotion close to happiness.

"What?"

"I'm having fun."

Mo glanced over at him. "Well, sure. So am I."

"No, what I mean is—" No, he thought, don't say it. He shrugged. "Nothing. It's not important."

She stopped and faced him, her arms crossed over her chest. "What did you say about people who don't finish sentences? I'm not moving till I hear it."

Matt felt awkward now, but he scratched his head and gave it a try. "It's just that, I usually travel alone. And this trip wasn't supposed to be anything more than research. It was a career move, really."

"I thought it was to be your honeymoon. Yours and Kay's."

"That, too." He frowned. "I owe Kay an apology when we get back."

"For what exactly? If you don't mind my asking."

"No, it's all right. For…" He searched for the words. What he was experiencing was difficult to pin down; he was in the realm of emotions here, and he wasn't well versed in that territory. But Mo was easy to talk to, and safe somehow.

"For not taking her feelings into account," he said finally. "For treating something as important as a honeymoon as, well, as business. I think she tried to tell me that when she called off the wedding."

"I see. But, the trip…I mean, haven't you been to all these places before? And isn't it still business?"

"Of course, but being with you makes it unlike the other times. I mean," he went on, "you've never been here before and I guess I'm seeing things through your eyes. You're fun to travel with."

He hadn't allowed himself a lot of fun. Work, not relationships, had ruled his adult life. But not at the present. Something about the way Mo experienced the world—head-on and with enthusiasm—was contagious. He wasn't sure when his priorities had changed, but now the trip was about giving Mo a wonderful time and watching her face while she did.

"Anyhow," he said, "it's you that makes the difference."

"Really?" Mo gave a little embarrassed shrug at his compliments. "Well, I'm happier than a pig in slop. Now that I've finally gotten myself across the Atlantic, I know I'll be back. Often, if I can swing it. But for now, it's good that one of us has traveled a lot before, so we don't wind up lost all the time."

"If you'll keep on supplying the enthusiasm, I'll supply the experience."

"I guess we make a pretty good combination, huh."

He met her gaze deliberately. "Yes," he said quietly, "a pretty good combination."

He watched her face as both of their last comments still hung in the air. Mo's eyes were wide-awake now, and softly vulnerable. She and Matt stood there, in the middle of a busy Paris street, with people walking and jostling on either side of them, but he felt as though they were in their own private world.

This sense of closeness and connection to her made his heart lurch. It was more than simply sexual attraction, although that was always there. But just *what* it was, he had no idea. He wanted to say something, but he didn't know what.

Instead, he took her hand, and she didn't draw it away. It was small and smooth and cool in his palm. He laced their fingers together and smiled. "Friends can hold hands, can't they?"

"I...guess so," she said slowly.

"You know, this friendship concept is all right."

For a quick second he thought he saw disappointment on her face at his use of the words *friend* and *friendship*. But, no, he'd probably imagined it, he decided in the next moment, because she favored him with one of her sunny smiles and said, "Absolutely. Friendship. The best."

They spent the rest of the day walking around the Ile de la Cité and Ile Saint-Louis, the two islands at the heart of Paris. As Matt pointed out the monuments—the Eiffel Tower, the Grand Palais, the Louvre—Mo pointed out the people. He smiled along with her at the poignant sight of an extremely wrinkled elderly woman with a very young child sitting in her lap, both of them fishing in the river. They stopped and watched an argument between a bearded man carrying a birdcage and a hefty woman brandishing a long baguette, the spittle flying as both screamed at the top of their lungs.

When a midget in a beret and a silver eye patch slyly offered postcards of nineteenth-century pornography, Mo insisted on looking through the selection, then glanced up at Matt with raised eyebrows. "Boy, things haven't changed much, have they?"

"Let me see," he said, reaching for them.

"Nope." Mo handed the postcards back to the little man with the eye patch, blushing slightly as she said, *"Merci."* Then she grabbed Matt's arm. "Too corrupting. Come along."

When they passed the magnificent Notre-Dame Cathedral and Matt was in lecture mode on all the Gothic carvings, Mo spied two nuns near the curb, licking ice-cream cones. "I want what they have," she said, pointing.

"A religious life?"

She giggled. "Ice cream."

"Your wish is my command."

They took a taxi to Berthillion, the home, he informed her, of the best in the world. Once there, they had to wait in line for a while. Finally, an extremely surly woman in a pink apron looked at them with one raised eyebrow. *"Oui?"*

Mo said, "Chocolate."

"Chocolat."

"No, wait," Matt interrupted, then turned to Mo. "Look, the thing about this place is that it's different. They make their ice cream from all kinds of fruits, whatever's in season. They're famous for it."

"That's nice. But I still want chocolate."

"Un moment, madame," he said to the lady who was now tapping her fingernails on the counter impatiently. "Mo, please. Trust me. It's delicious. Think of it—ice cream made from rhubarb, black currants, figs, kumquats."

She crossed her arms over her chest, as though declaring war. "Sorry. I want chocolate and nothing you're saying is making me change my mind."

"Were you like this as a child?"

"You know, Matt, it's really not okay to try to force people to eat things they don't want."

He glared at her, then relaxed. He was doing it again, wasn't he? Still—

"All right," he said. "We'll get two cones. One chocolate, and one fresh melon. One taste, that's all I ask. Are we agreed?"

"You are the pushiest man..." She shrugged. "Okay,

as long as you don't take my rejection personally. This has nothing to do with you.''

''Promise.''

Matt didn't know why he was pressing so hard—and yes, he was taking it personally, he knew it—but it just seemed important to him that she find *something* he recommended worthwhile.

When the cones were served, and they'd left the shop, Mo held the melon-flavored one in her hand, looked at it as though it had horns, then gave the ice cream a small swipe with her tongue. The look of surprise on her face, followed by a grin and a thumbs-up gesture, let him know the treat passed muster. He felt his chest filling with pride, although he wasn't quite sure why. About time, he thought silently.

''You're right, I'm wrong,'' Mo said graciously. ''It's really good.''

She went to work on the cone with her usual gusto, but after several nibbles, the scoop of ice cream fell to the ground. ''Oh, no,'' Mo said, bending down with her napkin to scoop it up.

''I'll get you another one,'' he said, kneeling beside her to help.

''It's my own fault. I'm always in a hurry.'' She mopped at the mess. ''It's why I trip all the time and drop things and get stains on everything. I don't take enough time.'' She raised her head and gazed at him, the look on her face one of such sweet, sorrowful self-reproach he wanted to grab her and kiss her till she stopped chastising herself, and then kiss her some more.

Instead, he went into the shop for more napkins, wondering how the hell he was expected to have such a lively, laugh-filled day with someone like Mo, and not want her.

Friendship was all well and good, but he wished someone would tell that to his body.

At breakfast on their last day in Paris, Mo looked up from her third croissant and said, "What do you think about me taking over? For today, I mean."

"Excuse me?" Matt set down his coffee cup.

She folded her elbows on the table and gazed at him earnestly. "Most people on a honeymoon can't afford all this—" she made a vague waving gesture with her hand "—four-star dining and class-A surroundings, now, can they?"

"I suppose not."

"So, if you'll translate, we can talk to a bunch of people and find some fun affordable places for your book and check them out."

Matt considered her suggestion, then nodded slowly. "You're right. I should have thought of that, and I'm the expert." More and more, he appreciated her resourceful mind. "I'm game. Where do we start?"

Mo's plan involved them talking to the hotel maids, then to a young, long-haired waiter, who conferred with a chef's assistant and a potato peeler. A Vietnamese busboy and a Jamaican pot scrubber joined in the conversation.

Away from the hotel, Mo and Matt chatted with various couples at sidewalk cafés—all of them young and not particularly affluent. Rather, Mo did the chatting and Matt translated her ebullience as well as he could. After a few of these conversations, he was amazed to find himself loosening up, actually exchanging some spirited comments with several of the people—strangers all, but pleasant strangers. Soon he and Mo had a list of small, offbeat restaurants and after-hours clubs.

On this final day in Paris, Matt agreed to put away his need to lead in an orderly fashion and let Mo call the shots. Hers was a world of improvisation.

They walked and took taxis all over the city, Mo stopping whenever the mood struck her and insisting they investigate some small shop or walk down an alleyway that "called" to her. At each eating place, Mo assessed the atmosphere, Matt the menu and the smells emanating from the kitchen, always getting only a couple of notes scribbled in his book before Mo grabbed his hand and announced it was time to move on.

Late in the afternoon, they wound up at a small outdoor bistro on the Left Bank, located in a secret garden between two eighteenth-century mansions. There, too full for a proper meal, they sat at an umbrella table and nibbled hors d'oeuvres and drank wine. They made up stories about the history of the two buildings and, as they had all day, laughed a lot.

As the sun began to set and the sky changed from bright to midnight blue, a sudden flash of lightning illuminated the dark garden.

"Oh," Mo said. "Look!"

"At what?" He couldn't take his eyes off her.

"It's raining. I love rain."

She got up from her chair, stepped out from under the umbrella and put her face up to the sky.

Matt stared, aware that right then, he wanted to do nothing but savor the moment. To dine in Paris, cooled by the rain, watching Mo lifting her face to the sky, it was exhilarating. She was so special—so alive! He wanted to join her, to pick her up and twirl her around. Her skin, her hair, the shining gaiety in her eyes, she called out to his senses as though he were under a spell.

Still, it was raining. He grabbed her hand and made her sit down. "You'll get soaked."

"It was only a light sprinkle."

But the sprinkles had done their work. The front of her blouse was dampened and clung to her. Her nipples stood out beneath the damp fabric, impossible to ignore.

Not that he wanted to. He swallowed a sudden infusion of saliva. If she expected him to ignore her, he was in deep trouble here. Or she was.

As Mo brushed out her hair with a hairbrush from her purse, she said, "Time to hit the nightspots."

The dark, smoke-filled basement club was filled with bodies writhing on the dance floor and superloud music pouring from the speakers. Mo found herself keeping time to the music from the moment they walked in the place.

"This is perfect," she said. "All of it. I don't understand any of the lyrics, but who cares, right?" She grabbed Matt's hand. "Dance with me?"

"Shouldn't we get a table first?"

"Nope."

He hesitated a moment more, and Mo thought that maybe he didn't like to dance. Or couldn't.

"Unless you'd rather not," she added.

A small smile played around his sensuous lips. "Oh, I'd rather. Most definitely."

The drums and bass were cranked way up, the beat pulsed through Mo's bloodstream. She loved to dance, loved to let go. Matt probably didn't let go on the dance floor.

But he surprised her. The man could move, really move, with an abandon she hadn't seen in him yet. Except when they'd kissed in the zoo.

The beat was hot and Mo felt in total sync with Matt, whirling, swaying, keeping time without speaking, coming together and parting, all kinds of unspoken messages dangling in the air between them. A fine sheen of perspiration glowed all over his face, and his dark eyes were lit with an inner fire, when they weren't closed in what seemed an expression of bliss.

Then the driving music changed to something slow and dreamy. As though they'd been choreographed, she and Matt came together, him pulling her into his arms, lifting her hands to his shoulders and wrapping his own around her waist. Without thinking, she rested her head against his chest. His shirt was silk, and her cheek rubbed against the soft fabric as they danced.

Neither of them spoke for a while. His heartbeat thrummed in her ear. She felt magical, warmed, cared for.

And turned on. Oh, yes, most definitely turned on. The way they moved together on that wooden floor, each somehow knowing what the other would do before they did it, with matching rhythms. It was, Mo thought dreamily, like really good sex.

"Oh," she said.

"What?" Matt murmured in her ear.

She glanced up at him, couldn't meet his eyes, and rested her cheek on his chest again. "I was just thinking about what a good dancer you are."

"Surprised?"

"Yes, as a matter of fact."

"Good."

She glanced up at him again. "Why 'good'?"

"I like to think you don't know everything about me."

"Well, I don't, of course."

"Good."

What did he mean? she wondered, and then for a while she stopped caring. She lost herself in sensation. The hard planes of Matt's body and the smell of him— the remnants of his lime-scented after-shave, the very maleness of him. The perspiring bodies around them, the faint sweet smell of cigarettes. The pulse of the music, a woman's voice sighing in what had to be the sexiest language in the world.

Matt was feeling it, too; she knew it. His arm tightened around her even more. As he pressed into her, she was aware of his arousal against her stomach, and something about that felt wonderful.

And...not quite right.

She pulled away. "I think we have enough for the book, right? I think we should go back to the hotel."

His lids lowered and a half smile played on one corner of his mouth. "Sounds good to me."

He leaned toward her, his mouth very close, too close. He was going to kiss her.

She placed her hand against his chest. "I can go myself if you'd like to stay here. I mean, if you're not tired, the way I am."

Mo was being evasive again, and she hated that. But if this went on any longer, they'd wind up in bed, no avoiding it, and something deep in her still didn't feel right about that. She tried to remember why, but she was having trouble. Something about a man with silver eyes...and her romantic destiny. However, that inner warning voice was pretty faint at the moment. She was almost ready not to listen to it, she was so swept up in the essence of this man. Almost.

"Matt, I'm sorry. I need to be alone."

"Alone?"

"Yes. We have a pretty early departure in the morning, don't we? So, I need to get some sleep."

"Alone," he repeated.

She swallowed. She hated not dealing with this now, but she couldn't think with Matt around. "Yes. Alone."

His expression turned thunderous. That frown of his could probably stop an army from advancing. "Fine," he said, pulling away abruptly. "But you're not going back alone. Not at night."

"But—"

"Don't even think it. Come on."

The scowl on his face was pretty awesome. She figured the best thing she could do was to go along.

She would lock the door between their rooms that night.

Not that she was afraid of what Matt might do.

It was her own actions she was uncertain about.

9

"Many *bambini* stay," the manager apologized with appropriate bowing and raising of regretful eyebrows. "Every *letto*, bed, taken. Many *famiglie* with *bambini*, *si*?"

Mo and Matt were in Venice, in the lobby of a wonderful hotel with a balcony overlooking the canal. And there seemed to be a problem with the booking. A big problem.

She and Matt had been polite but strained since the night before in Paris and on the plane today. She felt uncomfortable, and he was his old detached self.

Mo had been listening for the past few minutes as the manager, in a mixture of broken English and Italian, translated by Matt, explained that there had been terrible water damage in the honeymoon suite, making it unfit for habitation. Only one other room was available, with one bed, but *grazie a Dio* a double bed.

"*Miscusi signore, potrebbe raccomandarmi un altro hotel?*" Matt said.

"What?" Mo said. "What did you just say?"

"I asked him to recommend another hotel."

"*No, no, Signor Vining, Venezia e' al completo, e' la stagione estiva!*"

"What did he say?"

"He said the town's all full."

She was surprised to feel a small rush of excitement at the thought of being forced to share a room with Matt that evening, but she immediately crossed her arms to try to dampen that rush. "Ask him about another room."

"He already said there isn't one."

"Yes, but there has to be something—a maid's room, a linen closet, something."

Matt stared at her for a moment, then turned back to the manager, a short, balding man with a huge mustache. Another torrent of Italian, complete with hand gestures and raised eyebrows, followed. After several back-and-forth exchanges, Matt turned to her, shaking his head and obviously trying not to smile.

"What?" she said again.

"I asked is there a maid's room. He replied, 'Excuse me, sir, why do you need another room? Is it not a honeymoon for you and your new wife?' and I said, 'Yes, but I need a room to work in. I'm writing a book.' Then he said that was a very sad thing, to be writing a book on your honeymoon."

The manager was gazing at her with great sorrow, shaking his head and rolling his eyes. *"Americani,"* he said sadly. *"Così buffoni."*

Mo didn't need a translation for that one.

The little man let fly with another flood of words. *"Una nuova moglie, e anche così' bella. Se non to dispiace il mio dire, una moglie di cui ogni uomo sarebbe orgoglioso, e mol tial trisarebbero daccordo—bellissima!"*

"Grazie."

"What?" Mo asked.

"He complimented me on my choice of wives."

"There was more."

"You're beautiful, he said. I should be grateful to have you. I believe I was being lectured on the dangers of ignoring a new wife."

She narrowed her lids. "You're enjoying this, aren't you?"

Matt shrugged, but the gleam of laughter in his eyes was hard to miss. She much preferred it to his earlier coolness. "Hey, I'm doing the best I can here."

"How about a cot?"

He leaned an elbow casually against the marble reception desk. "Many families, he said, remember? Many *bambini*, so no extra beds. Besides, what would I use as an excuse?"

"I don't know," she said, throwing her hands up in the air. "You're the writer, make something up."

"Sorry. I only write about food. Fiction isn't my strong suit."

"You did fine with the book story."

"It was all I had in my arsenal."

"Well, then, tell him I'm sick. Or I have my— Oh, forget it. I don't know."

Mo chewed her bottom lip and stared up at the ceiling, hoping for inspiration. Since that first night in Paris, when she'd had too much wine and realized she was jealous, since the last night in Paris, when they'd danced and she realized her attraction to him was getting stronger and stronger, since, well, all along, really—this scene had been coming. There was somehow a sense of inevitability about the whole thing. As though it was fated. She could feel it closing in on her, like ocean waves too strong to fight.

At least, up to now, she'd been able to swim away. They'd been in separate rooms, or in public, when the subject of that chemistry between them had come up.

Now, short of throwing a tantrum and walking out of here with her bags, she would be sharing not just a room, but a bed, a very private bed, with the gentleman this very night. And the next. And the next.

He couldn't have planned this, could he? The whole thing was too corny, too shifty, too *manipulative,* for someone like Matt. Still, to be sure, she turned and glared at him accusingly.

At the moment, he would win a poker tournament for all the expression he wore on his face. Noncommittal to the max. "So," Matt said. "What do you want to do?"

She chewed her lip again while she considered, then said, "I don't know. I'm going for a walk."

"But—"

She waved her hands at him. "Why don't you work on your book, okay? I'll be back later. I gotta get out of here."

He stared at her as though trying to figure her out. Then, frowning, he glanced down at their luggage, still gathered on the floor in front of the desk. "Well, I do need to put in a couple of hours on my notes. I haven't been keeping up with them."

"Gee, how awful," she said sarcastically. "Too much fun, I suppose."

He allowed a small crack of a smile. "Something like that. But, look, don't go off just yet. Venice is filled with lots of alleyways and streets with no signs and that go nowhere. You'll get lost. If you wait till I'm finished—"

"I'm a big girl. I'll manage."

"Mo, really—"

"Matt, really," she said, imitating his tone of voice.

He got it then, and cut off his lecture abruptly. Removing his elbow from the desk, he stood up straight.

"Mo, believe it or not, I'm sorry it's working out this way, but I didn't plan it."

She emitted a sigh and nodded. "I know," she said grudgingly. "But that doesn't mean I'm happy about it."

A spasm of hurt crossed his face quickly, replaced immediately by that familiar closed-off look. "Am I that difficult to take?"

"Of course not. You're too *easy* to take. That's the problem." She covered her mouth with her hand then, wishing the words hadn't sprung out of her quite that way. She'd been responding to that fleeting glimpse of hurt feelings, instead of monitoring her speech. For a change.

"Forget I said that."

His sudden grin was wide and smug. "Yes, ma'am."

All compassion for him vanished in an instant. "I'm out of here."

As she turned to go, he grabbed her arm. "Wait. At least, will you take this?" He snatched up a street map from the desk, where the manager was avidly trying to follow the conversation. He handed her the map. "Maybe this will help."

"Sure," she replied, managing to leave out the fact that she was hopeless with maps and had never had anything even approaching a sense of direction. A person was born with that one or a person wasn't. Still, she always found her way back. Eventually.

Grabbing her purse and stuffing the map inside, Mo walked to the front door, then turned back one more time. "Oh, yeah, is the big dinner tonight?"

"No, tomorrow."

"Good."

"But I know a place for this evening—"

"Of course you do," she interrupted him. "But

please, pretty please, make it small. And casual. With simple, easy-to-digest food.'' Patting her stomach, she added, ''It can't take too much more.''

''What? The original junk-food queen is having tummy problems?''

''I guess it's time to pass the crown to someone else.''

He nodded. ''All right. I'll take care of it.''

''Thanks,'' she said with a small forgiving smile. She wasn't used to feeling angry, and, really, how could she be angry at Matt? It was the situation that was bothering her, not him.

Matt smiled back at her, and the manager, beaming at the two of them, said something flowery and emotional. Then he kissed his fingertips and released the kiss into the air.

Mo eyed Matt warily, almost afraid to hear what had just been said.

He deadpanned, ''Signor Mazzeo assures us it's normal for newlyweds to fight. We'll make up later, in our small, cozy room. Venice is a magic place—'' he paused ''—for lovers.''

Matt's brown-eyed gaze was warmly amused and filled with promise, and at that moment, Mo knew she was in trouble.

The deep, deep kind.

Matt looked at his watch again, then glanced out the room's one small window. The view was of a narrow alleyway, but if you craned your neck you could see part of the street in front of the hotel. No Mo. She'd been gone nearly three hours. Night was closing in. Where the hell was she?

With a curse of disgust, Matt grabbed a jacket and, leaving his notes scattered all over the small table, tore down the three flights of stairs. Once out the hotel's front door, he gazed all around him. He could choose one of five directions to go in; Venice was like that. With hands on hips, he peered down each street for any sign of her. Damnit, he thought, he didn't even know if Mo had the name of the hotel written down. He should have insisted—

"*Buona sera, signorina,*" said a man's voice nearby, and someone who sounded exactly like Mo replied, "*Buona sera, signore.*" Matt turned around to see Mo coming out of an alleyway, scooting past the leering man who had spoken to her. Although several bundles were in her arms, she was managing to nibble on an ice-cream cone.

As she came toward Matt, he observed her outfit: all her hair was tucked up under a baseball cap and she wore a short, swingy green skirt and matching T-shirt and sandals. Which was strange, because when she'd left she'd been wearing jeans and a blouse and sneakers.

"Hi," she said, crunching on some more of her cone and coming to a stop a couple of feet in front of him.

"Hello." He made it casual, easy; he was damned if he was going to tell her he'd been worried.

"You were right. I got hopelessly lost. And I slipped when this guy who owns a jewelry store was watering his plants. I fell pretty hard—" She showed him a scraped elbow, then took another swipe at the ice cream. "And I got all soaked, but everyone was so nice to me. I gave them the jeans and got beads for my mom and some other stuff for my nephews and this outfit." She twirled around, the skirt lifting and ballooning slightly as she did. "Like it?"

He swallowed. Her long, shapely legs could make a

blind man weep. "Very nice. Are you sure you're all right?"

"Tip-top. But my watch is ruined. What time is it?"

"Seven. How did you get back? Did you use the map?"

"It got soaked, too. Not that I had the least idea how to read it." She shrugged and licked at the last of the ice cream. "I asked people."

"But you don't speak the language."

Grinning, she shifted a couple of packages to the other arm. "Yeah, I didn't understand a word, but some of the gestures were kind of ballpark, directions-wise, and well, here I am."

"Let me take those." He reached for one of the bags but she stepped away, as though not wanting to place herself within touching distance.

"No, it's okay, I'll just put them in the room. You probably want to eat dinner, huh?"

"It appears you already have."

"Just a little appetizer-type gelato." She tossed the rest of the cone into a trash container. "I'll take this stuff upstairs, then I'll be right down."

Matt sat at a little outdoor table and ordered a *martini bianco* while he waited. He still felt a little tense. Mo's mood, on the other hand, had seemed relaxed, if somewhat impersonal.

He drummed his fingers on the table. What had she decided to do about the room? he wondered. Whatever she did decide, it was up to her, and that was all there was to it. He'd made his interest in her known more than a couple of times. He was willing and available; she couldn't have missed that message. Any more on his part and he would appear—and be—a fool.

He nodded to himself, his position clear. He would no longer pursue her. If Mo wanted him, she'd have to make the first move.

10

When she came down, Matt still couldn't figure out her state of mind. The two of them headed off while Mo chattered happily about everything she'd seen that day.

"Shops and cafés and homes, and these wonderful cobblestoned streets. Everybody has flowers, geraniums mostly, in boxes under their windows. There are lots of trees and bushes, but no grass, you know? It's funny. And everywhere you go, there's the water. Stop for a minute," she said as they passed a small clothing store, its owner closing up for the day.

"*Buona sera*," said the store owner.

"*Buona sera*," Mo said with a smile, perused the window for a moment, then turned to Matt. She put her hand on his arm, then withdrew it quickly. "What do you smell?"

"The ocean."

"Okay, what *don't* you smell?"

"Is this a trick question?"

"Gasoline. There's no gas smell. You're not allowed to have cars or buses or trucks here, right? So there's no city smell, like we're used to in San Francisco. All you get is this kind of faint stale-fish odor that you have near an ocean. And the humidity has a...damp smell to it, too. And listen."

She paused, then whispered, "See how quiet it is? There's all that non-noise of traffic, so you hear people laughing and talking, and birds chirping, and water lapping against the sides of the canals. But it's quiet. Because there're no cars."

Closing his eyes, Matt made himself listen. She was right. The city of Venice *was* quiet, and it was refreshing. He'd been here five or six times before, and had never really noticed the smells and sounds. Now he couldn't help noticing them, thanks to Mo. She really was extraordinarily perceptive.

They walked some more. Mo went on talking, but he noticed a strained quality; it was as though she was afraid of there being too much silence between them, and was babbling to fill the emptiness.

"I can't count how many bridges I crossed. I mean, there are so many bridges! And the alleyways are so narrow, sometimes you have to practically turn sideways to pass someone."

"Did you get pinched?"

She snorted. "Better believe it. And each time I turned around to give the guy a piece of my mind, I could never tell who it was. It's a stupid tradition."

"But a very old one."

"Yeah, well. Old is not necessarily good. Oh, look!"

She pointed. In the distance was San Marco Square. Mo ran ahead of him, toward the enormous plaza, her arms stretched out like a child pretending to fly. All around her, pigeons scattered and flew into the darkening night sky. Mo twirled and laughed, then turned to face him and laughed again.

"I've seen this place in so many movies! The huge church and all the tables here and there and all the people. It's just like I thought it would look, only better!"

He nodded, feeling some of her enthusiasm shooting into his bloodstream. Yes, Saint Mark's was special. Tonight, the square was illuminated by the soft amber lights on the huge cathedral, reflecting off the other buildings and cobblestones and the faces of diners at the many cafés, giving the whole scene the appearance of being made of gold.

Mo got to choose the café, as Matt was of the opinion that all the food in the square was decent. She picked the one right in the center of the action. As they sat down, she couldn't stop smiling and looking around her. Venice. She was in Venice!

Music came from four different orchestras playing four different kinds of music and alternating sets so as not to interfere with each other or the diners' ears. At any moment they might hear jazz, then American pop standards, then Vivaldi, and all the sounds bounced off the walls of the surrounding buildings, creating a natural stereophonic effect.

It was another magical night on this perfect trip, Mo thought. Except, of course, for that slight tension in the air. She and Matt had unfinished business—the room situation—but both seemed reluctant to deal with finishing it. He had been unusually quiet, while she'd been hopping and skipping and prattling for dear life.

Boy, it was hard not to deal with something that wouldn't go away, no matter how hard you tried to make it do just that. Take that afternoon, on her journey through the streets of this city that she'd been reading and dreaming about all her life. Even as she oohed and aahed over what she was seeing and smelling and hearing, a lot of her head for a lot of the afternoon had been taken up with fantasies, steamy, X-rated stuff, about the night to come. And each time she invented one, she would berate herself for allowing her imagination to go off in that direction.

But fantasies were one thing, reality was something different. You didn't have to go to bed with a person just because you were sharing a room. Did you? Unless, of course, that was what you wanted to do anyway. Did she want to?

There was something more niggling at her, something real important—about another layer of feelings—yet when she tried to focus on what that was, it whisked away like a feather caught in a back draft.

At any rate, she and Matt were due for some sort of showdown. Okay, a discussion at least. But...not yet. Coward, she called herself silently. You got it, she answered.

"Excuse me?" Mo realized that Matt had been speaking to her and she'd been off in la-la land. "What did you say?"

"I said we're meeting the photographer for pictures tonight, after dinner."

"Oh, where?"

"Well, when she and I spoke earlier, she suggested a night gondola ride. She's setting it up now."

"Oh." An instant fantasy flashed through Mo's mind—she and Matt sitting side by side in the moonlight, his arm around hers in the cozy darkness. The air is warm as they pass under a bridge. Shadows, then darkness. His hand finds its way to her—

"I've arranged for us to meet her at ten," Matt said, "a short walk from here."

"Who?" She was in a daze and had to snap out of it. Now. "Oh, yes, the pictures. For the book."

"I assume that's all right," he said politely.

"Of course."

So, an hour later, Mo found herself in what—once again—felt like a scene from a movie. The graceful gondola and the olive-skinned Italian man at the helm. The dark sky and the moon. The sound of lapping water rustling through it all. The man and the woman trying not to be attracted to each other.

The photographer, Angelina, was shorter, younger and rounder than Mo, with enormous gold hoop earrings dangling past her shoulders. She was also a little on the hyper side. Mo kept wanting to giggle as Angelina danced around, arranging her lights and directing her subjects in various dramatic poses, as though she were Fellini.

Finally, Mo and Matt settled themselves on the cushioned bench at one end of the gondola, while Angelina encouraged them to snuggle up ever closer. Mo leaned her head against Matt's chest and felt his arm come around her shoulders, but lightly, as though not ready to commit to actual touching. The flash went off several times, interspersed with *"Fantastico!"* and *"Bello!"* from the photographer.

When she insisted the newlyweds kiss, Mo said "I don't think so tonight," at the same time Matt said, "We already have a lot of those."

They looked at each other and smiled self-consciously. Neither of them wanted any physical intimacy, it was obvious. Mo felt a small dart of hurt, but told herself to cut it out. Matt was behaving, being a good sport. A gentleman.

After the picture-taking session was over, and they'd said their goodbyes to Angelina, Mo assumed they were done. She was in the act of pushing herself up from the seat, when the oarsman pushed them off from the dock instead.

She sat back down with a thump. "Oof."

"You all right?" Matt said.

"Sure, but why are we moving?"

"Probably because we're on the water in a seagoing vessel," he said dryly.

"No, no, I mean, I didn't know we were actually going on a nighttime gondola ride."

Matt spoke to the gondolier, who answered with a languid shrug and a rush of words. Matt turned back to Mo. "He says we paid for his time, we might as well get our money's worth."

They were away from the dock now, moving slowly through the canal. The soft splashing of the water as they glided along was gentle, lulling. It felt wonderful.

"But I'm not sure—" She stopped.

"You're not sure of what?"

His question lingered in the air for a couple of heartbeats. It was, after all, the problem in a nutshell.

"Not sure if I want to go on a gondola ride," she said finally, in a voice that sounded, even to her ears, petulant.

"Then we tell him to turn around," Matt said stiffly. "You call it."

Sighing, she eased herself back till she was staring up at the night sky. The more time she took to think about what she wanted to do, the farther away from the dock they drew. Eventually, they turned into another canal, a wider, darker one, far away now from the lights. Mo's mind drifted with the gondola's movement.

The moon was three-quarters full, the sky cloudless. Stars shone above, looking the way stars looked all over the world, and Mo understood then that she had avoided dealing decisively with the room situation all day because she already knew what she wanted to do, deep down in the inner recesses of her soul. She wanted Matt. Craved him. It was that simple, really.

Wasn't it? Shouldn't it be?

Matt sat straight, rigid even, next to her, staring ahead. She gazed at his profile—stern and classic, the planes of his face harsh in the faint light of the moon and the occasional street lamp along the canal. He was making no moves toward her, was in fact being specifically neutral.

Propping herself up on one elbow, Mo laid a gentle hand on his arm. He jumped slightly and turned to face her.

"It's a beautiful night, isn't it?" she said.

He said nothing.

"It would be a shame to waste this ride." She brought her face closer; his eyes glowed like banked coals.

"Are we wasting this ride?" he asked.

"So far." Tentatively, her hand found its way around his neck and she brushed her fingers lightly against the nape. "What do you think?"

"About what?"

He wasn't making this easy for her, was he? And Mo wasn't real skilled at seduction. Oh, well, you never know till you try it, she counseled herself silently.

"What do you think about giving your, uh, pretend wife a real kiss?"

His indrawn breath was the only reaction he showed her. "I think it sounds just fine."

Leaning closer to her reclining body, he said, his voice hoarse, "More than fine. It sounds like heaven."

He covered her mouth with his, cupping one cheek in his hand as he did. At the moment of connection, she heard a low moan. She wasn't sure if it was from her or from him. Closing her eyes, she let the sensation of him wash through her.

His mouth was soft, yet insistent. He stroked her face with his fingertips, then caught her chin and angled her head slightly and kissed her again, more deeply this time. His mouth did wondrous, delicious things to hers. She was being savored, appreciated, *tasted*, on many levels by a connoisseur. She was in the hands of an expert, and the contrast between this supersensual Matt and the one she'd met only a few days ago was, again, mind-boggling.

Heat raced through her bloodstream and brought warmth to her cheeks, but there was no thought; she turned into a quivering mass of sensations. He turned her head again, changing the angle of his mouth on hers, and this time his tongue burst through with a strong, moist surge. The fire that shot through her veins surprised her with its sudden intensity. Her tongue met his and she felt the movement of his hand over her shoulders and toward the front of her shirt.

Hold it, she thought. Wait. Things were heating up a little faster than she was prepared for. Especially as there was a gondolier practically right over their heads.

"Matt," Mo said softly, breaking off the kiss.

"What?" He turned his attention to her ear, making her quiver some more.

"We have a witness."

"He's probably used to it."

"I'm not."

"Then how about if I tell him to head back?" He kissed her neck, then all along her collarbone, sending small shivers up and down her spine and to the tips of her breasts. "So we can get to our room quickly," he added in a whisper.

Muscles clenched deep inside and she exhaled loudly, and audibly. "Yes," she said.

Matt lifted his head and gazed at her through passion-glazed eyes. "You're sure you want to do this," he said in a self-assured way that let her know he didn't really expect an answer—her body's response to him had been answer enough.

But, why, oh, why had he asked her? After half a beat, she said, "Sure I'm sure."

Her slight hesitation made some of the glaze leave his eyes. "Mo..."

"Yes."

"I'm—we're—about to pass all reasonable behavior, and I want you to be *very* sure. One hundred percent sure, as a matter of fact."

She played with the collar of his shirt. "Would you accept ninety-eight percent?"

Sitting up, Matt raked his hair with trembling fingers. "God almighty. For once, couldn't you have lied?"

"Okay. One hundred percent."

He muttered a succinct curse, wiped his face with his hand, then studied her as though she were a new kind of puzzle. "All right. What is the other two percent about?"

"Stuff rattling around in my head." She couldn't seem to meet his gaze. "Like, I still wonder if I'm a substitute for Kay."

He heaved a sigh of exasperation. "Mo, Mo, Mo," he said, shaking his head. "What in the hell am I going to do with you?" He grabbed her by the shoulders. "Listen and listen carefully. That Kay theory is nonsense, utter nonsense. This—you and me—has nothing to do with anything but the moonlight and an undeniable attraction that we both feel, and you are just as caught up in it as I am. Don't say you're not.''

"I won't," she said quickly. "Promise."

He nodded and gentled his hold on her shoulders, absently massaging the material of her shirt. Then he ran one of his thumbs across her lower lip and offered her a sexy now-where-were-we? half smile. "Does that take care of the stuff in your head?"

"Well, there's the silver-eyed man, which is why I came here in the first place. I'm supposed to be on my way to meet him."

"Nonsense," he said again, a little more sharply than before. "Do you honestly believe anyone can tell the future? And even if you do, what does this fire between us have to do with someone you haven't even met yet? Are you saving yourself for him? For some fantasy man?"

"No, no, of course not."

She felt foolish and very young at that moment, not at all womanly. Except for her body's reaction to Matt— there was nothing childish about that. She told herself to cut out all this silliness.

"I'm sorry," she said. "Forget I said anything. I'm a grown-up and we both know what's happening here. It's not like I'm a starry-eyed eighteen-year-old or anything." She was babbling, but she couldn't seem to stop herself. "I mean, it's not like either of us is expecting anything, you know, like commitment or love or anything like that—"

"Hold it," he interrupted.

"But—"

"Who said anything about love?"

"Not me," she said quickly. "Not me, I didn't."

Why, why, *why* had she used that word? Mo wondered, seeing that black furrow forming on Matt's face, the one that preceded one of his emotional shutdowns. And *where* had that word come from?

Matt sat up, his back ramrod straight. At his withdrawal, something deflated inside Mo. Don't go away, she wanted to say.

But what had she been expecting? Words assuring her that what they had together was more than just a physical thing? That it was somehow special? Different?

An act of—admit it, now—of love?

Lowering her head, she concentrated on her hands, folded in her lap. Matt spoke to the gondolier, and they reversed direction.

Neither of them said anything for a while. Mo couldn't help feeling wrong, somehow, uncomfortable in her skin. What was he thinking? He was angry, for sure. Well, of course he was. Who could blame him? Just what was going on here?

Love? Did she love him?

But…she'd never even considered it. She'd found him attractive, sexy, amusing, intelligent and good company, especially when he wasn't distanced or controlling. She felt affection and friendship for him, and sometimes when he looked at her a certain way, something funny and fluttery happened in the region of her heart.

But love?

She certainly hadn't been aware of anything like that. But then, her stupid head was always betraying her, either by encouraging her to leap blindly into strange new situations or neglecting to inform her that something pretty important was percolating. Obviously, in the area of self-awareness, she was about as clueless as you could get.

After a while, she put a hand on his arm. "Matt, I'm sorry."

"For what?"

"I'm not sure. For making something simple into something, well, complicated."

He stared out at the night, his jaw clenching and unclenching several times before he said, "The thing is, I don't believe in love. It's a foreign concept. Sorry, but there it is."

"But you were engaged to be married."

"If you remember my history and my mother's many husbands, you'll understand why I don't connect marriage and lasting love. The lessons we learn in childhood have a way of staying around permanently."

"Oh."

"I was career-oriented and so was Kay. We had some good times and things in common. I've never expected anything else from a relationship. Mostly, I guess, we each had...empty moments in our lives. I thought it could work. It seemed a good idea at the time."

He said this distractedly, without emotion, except for that underlying coldness. Some more time passed during which the only sound was the steady swish of the oar in the softly rippling water.

"God," Mo said finally. "That's so sad."

"Please, I don't need your pity."

"No, I mean, that's not a reason to marry."

"I don't think there's any reason to marry, really, unless there are children involved." His chuckle lacked any trace of humor. "Remember where I come from. Most marriages I see are a farce. It seems to me that love doesn't last."

"That kind of talk is even sadder than marrying someone to fill up space."

"So, you believe in all that romantic claptrap—the house, the kids, growing old together."

"I've seen it work, so I guess I do. Someday, at least."

"Well, I don't. Anyway, I am what I am, and I don't really want to sit here and philosophize on the nature of love and life. Okay?"

He looked out on the water and shook his head again. The rest of the ride passed in silence. When they pulled up to the dock, Matt helped her out of the gondola, then walked with her, his hands firmly in his pockets, back to the hotel.

They climbed the stairs slowly. At the door, Matt looked at her and said, "Sleep well."

"Where are you going?"

"If you think I'm spending the night with you in that room, you're crazy. I'll see you in the morning."

11

Matt's thoughts kept pace with his furious strides as he headed into the nighttime streets of Venice; his mind invented and discarded images as quickly as paper through a shredder.

Earlier, Mo had talked about seeing San Marco Square in the movies. Wasn't the whole evening like something out of a film? The one where the man walks through a foreign city at midnight, his hands in his pockets, his shoulders hunched, frustrated as all get out, and not a little confused, while a lovely woman sits in a hotel room, ambivalent, and also not a little confused, and looking sexy as hell while she does?

Well, if it wasn't a scene from a movie, it should have been.

Just where was he to sleep tonight? Maybe he could find a small *pensione*, a local YMCA, if they had them in Italy—he'd never needed to know before.

Even a park bench.

Because he was through playing his role in this farce; his and Mo's prospects, sexually speaking, were finished, done, terminated. One more time, one more pail of cold water had been thrown on his raging hormones. It had to be some kind of record.

Most of the small bed-and-breakfast places he passed

were full, others were dark. He knocked on one door that showed a light in a downstairs room, but someone had fallen asleep in front of the TV and they were *cosi' mortificati*, so sorry, there was nothing available.

As Matt turned a corner, one of Venice's ubiquitous cats meowed loudly and brushed up against his shin. He told it to scram in a harsh voice.

No. Absolutely no. He was not about to go back to that room and imitate another familiar scene from filmdom—the one where the man and woman share a bed, each of them spending a sleepless night with their backs to each other, maybe even one of them under the sheet, the other above it, to prevent temptation from taking over. Not when, once again, Matt had been driven almost senseless with desire that ended up going nowhere.

The door of a small bar was ajar as he passed it, so he went in and ordered a large Campari and soda at the bar. But the sounds of people, of clinking glasses and conversation and laughter, made him feel lonely more than anything, so he left after quickly tossing down the drink.

What a way to spend a honeymoon—even a phony one! The honeymoon from hell, that's what it was.

He stopped and stared at a park bench. It looked hard. And wet. And cold. A youngish couple, their arms around each other as they laughed softly, passed him. The woman's perfume drifted across his nostrils; it was strong, too strong, not like the scent Mo wore. He always meant to ask her just how you got lemon and roses to blend that way.

Not that he cared.

Mo. Maureen Flynn Czerny—he'd seen her full name on her passport. Maureen Flynn Czerny believed in love.

Love.

Of all the juvenile…irritating…fantasy-filled concepts. Absurd.

Several more *pensiones* later, Matt had to give in to the obvious. There was no room at the inn, except for his own. Well, fine, the night was nearly over. He would march into the room, get some blankets and sleep on the floor, as far from the bed as possible. Mo and he had two more nights in Venice before going on to Prague, and he would find other accommodations first thing in the morning.

When he reached the hotel, he eyed the lobby's couch briefly before shaking his head ruefully and heading upstairs. At the room, Matt opened the door quietly. He didn't want to wake Mo up—he absolutely refused to deal with the woman again that night. The interior was fairly dark, lit only by a faint stream of moonlight coming in from the terrace. In the far corner was the bed, piled with bedclothes, under which Mo slept the sleep of the untroubled.

He made his way to the bathroom in the dark, closing the door before he turned on the light. Washing up, he tried to ignore the familiar aroma of Mo's perfume in the small space. He looked through the mess of bottles and tubes and tissues that was on her side of the sink for a bottle of perfume, but there wasn't one.

Leaning on the sink, he stared into the mirror. His dark beard shadowed his jawline, his hair was tousled, his eyes were bloodshot. He really was tired. That was the truth.

And he wished like hell that Mo's scent didn't permeate every room she inhabited, even when she was no longer in it.

He removed his clothes, but kept on his T-shirt and briefs. Leaving the bathroom door open a little for light, he felt around in the closet for an extra blanket. There were none. Yawning, he eyed the generous mound of linens on the bed, with Mo under them. Maybe just one sheet and one pillow.

Quietly, he went over to the bed and pulled gently at the top cover. Mo didn't stir. He pulled at it a little more, half expecting a groan of protest. But instead of protesting, the lump collapsed.

Matt ripped the covers off the bed. There was no one there.

His heart began to beat more rapidly. Had the foolish, idiotic woman gone off again, into the night, unprotected? Good God, did she never learn?

"Matt?"

He jumped at the sound of his name whispered in the shadowed darkness. Gazing toward the balcony, he saw a murky silver moon with clouds covering it like gauze. And beneath the moon, against the terrace railing, was Mo. Her face was in shadow, but her hair stood out from her head like a soft nimbus, and her body underneath a filmy long nightgown was perfectly outlined by the moon's light. The curve of her breast, the swell of her hips, those long, perfectly shaped legs. Drawing in a breath, he couldn't stop himself from staring.

And then she ran toward him, her arms outstretched, and as though on automatic pilot, he gathered her to him. He reminded himself that he was still furious. With her? The situation? Who the hell knew? It didn't matter because his body didn't seem to care about his state of mind.

"Matt," she said, pulling his face down and planting quick kisses all over it. "Matt, I'm sorry. Did I act like a tease? Leading you on, and all? I hate that, I'm not like that."

Her lips left tiny jolts of electricity in their wake. "No, no," he managed to say. "I knew you weren't teasing."

"I'd like to take the evening back to the moment when I asked you to kiss me, and forget about what happened afterward. No more words." She placed her small hands on the sides of his face and gazed up at him. Her eyes were huge in the moonlight, her face pale. "Can we?"

"Oh, Mo," he whispered.

"Come," she said softly.

"Where?"

"Here." She grabbed his hand and led him over to the bed. With her other hand, she swept away the pile of bedclothes, leaving clean bare sheets and nothing more. Then she lay down and reached her arms up to him. "Come."

He gazed at her luscious form, lying prone on the white sheets. He'd been down this road once before earlier tonight, and he didn't think he could take another rise and fall, metaphorically and physically. He thought about saying something sardonic like, "Are you sure this time?" or "Even without love?," but couldn't seem to form the words.

Because even as a part of him whispered a warning not to trust what was happening and called him all kinds of fool, he knew, deep inside, that this time Mo wouldn't stop for anything. She wanted him as much as he wanted her, if that was possible.

He sat on the edge of the bed, his attention drawn to the rosy brown nipples showing under the gauze of her nightgown. He felt almost dizzy. Gathering her hands in his, he brought them to his chest and pressed her palms to his heated skin. His heart thudded rapidly; in fact, his entire body was shuddering now, and he wondered briefly if he was coming down with some kind of exotic fever. Why else would a woman—no, this woman—affect him so deeply?

"Dammit," he said. "Do you see what you do to me?"

Mo wanted to cry all of a sudden, at the intensity of the moment, and at the emotion jammed up in the back of her throat. Lord, Matt's face was just too unbearably masculine, those strong cheekbones shadowed and sexy in the moonlight, those nearly black eyes alive with banked passion, but still darkly mysterious.

"Yes," she said, because she saw what she did to him. His body was shaking; he was on the edge of tumbling off a cliff, taking her with him.

And when he swept her up in his arms and buried his face in her neck and groaned as though he'd been waiting for her for two hundred years, she knew that she'd have to toss away those few lingering doubts, or watch them burned to ashes in the fire to come.

Grabbing both her wrists, Matt pulled her arms upward, so they rested on the pillow above her head. Then he kissed her, hard, devouring her mouth, crushing her head against the pillow. His actions verged on being violent, and Mo felt a quick tremor of excited fear. But immediately afterward, she watched him get hold of himself and put brakes on the surging need he was so obviously experiencing—as was she.

With utmost gentleness, Matt released her wrists to slowly undress her. After removing his own clothes, he reached into his pants pocket and withdrew a silver foil packet.

Finally, with a look on his face that was as tender and

unguarded as any she'd seen, he bent over and kissed her.

But gently, this time, even though she could sense the effort it was costing him. For the first few moments, Mo felt a little shy. But, as though a silent signal had been given, she and Matt quickly abandoned the slow, almost tentative touches, and were soon caught up in a maelstrom of sensations.

His mouth made magical forays on every part of her, making her nipples harden, her flesh come alive, and the woman's place between her legs and up into her womb, cry with eagerness to be touched, to be loved, to be possessed.

He played her like a skilled guitarist—stroking, plucking, setting up a rhythm that she could do nothing but follow and lose herself in. The rhythm increased and she followed that, too, and then he was poised over her.

She opened for him and made him welcome, and he plunged into her with one powerful surge. He filled her up, and she felt as though she was welcoming something new and something familiar at the same time. As if a part of her that Mo hadn't known was missing was suddenly returned to her, and she cried for joy.

Matt froze his thrusting movement even though she felt him still hard, still pulsing. Balancing himself on one elbow, he caught up some of her tears on a fingertip. "Oh, Mo. Have I hurt you?"

"No, no, no. Sorry." She sniffled. "This is just... incredible and, well, I'm so emotional."

Wrapping her up in his arms, he hugged her to him, and she could hear his breath still coming out in quick desperate spurts. She hugged him tightly. The man kept astonishing her. If she'd thought him in the least bit stodgy or formal or distanced, tonight he was proving her very, very wrong.

She moved her hips to let him know that even though she was crying, he didn't have to stop doing what he was doing. He picked up on her cue instantly. Emitting a loud groan, Matt took up where he'd left off, with firm strokes of hard, potent, insistent male magic. Her hips and inner muscles responded, and then it was impossible to tell who was setting the rhythm and who was following.

As the jolt of her climax ripped through her, Matt checked his movement for a brief moment. Then, with a cry as ancient as days, he released his life force into her. They trembled and quaked and gasped until Mo had no more energy left to do anything but lie in Matt's arms.

Even with her brain fogged-up with an afterglow unlike anything she'd ever experienced, it was still functioning enough to know that yes, she loved him. Was in love with him. Amazing, really amazing, as amazing as the skill and sheer *intensity* Matt had brought to their coupling.

No way could that have happened, with all that *passion* and, well, *rapture*, without love.

On her part, anyway. What Matt felt, she had no way of knowing, and after their discussion earlier that evening, she imagined he wouldn't welcome her own revelation. Which was kind of sad, but not hopeless, was it?

The wise course would be to say nothing to him about her discovery. Nothing at all. She rarely did the wise thing, but this time, she had to.

After a while, Matt withdrew from her and, turning her so her back was to him, pulled her close. He cupped her breasts in his hands and expelled warm breath onto her neck.

"Well, now," he murmured in her ear, "this is more what a honeymoon is supposed to be like." And with the next breath, she could tell he was asleep.

She did not join him immediately. Dazed and sated and exhausted, she allowed herself a brief moment to wonder just what he'd meant by that last remark.

And then she decided not to read anything into it. Snuggling herself even closer to his long, lean frame, Mo joined Matt in dreamland.

12

They made love again sometime in the middle of the night, and again as dawn broke in the sky. Matt couldn't seem to get enough of her. His passion for her astonished him, as did the way she seeped into him on all levels when their bodies were joined. He could feel those walls of privacy he kept around himself becoming thinner with each hour spent in Mo's arms. He wasn't quite sure what to do without the walls; this was uncharted territory, and he felt apprehensive about what would happen next.

They were awakened by a soft knock on the door announcing breakfast. Soon, Matt and Mo were sitting up in bed, sipping cappuccinos and munching on *ciambelles*, soft, warm doughnuts coated with sugar. Mo declared these actually better than Winchell's glazed buttermilk.

She seemed slightly subdued this morning, although a slightly subdued Mo would appear energetic on anyone else. He thought about asking her if she had any regrets or if the night had been as unique, as special for her as it had been for him. But every time he framed the question in his mind, it sounded too damned vulnerable. Or, at least, he decided, too serious for such a fine morning.

Instead, he held her close and licked scattered sugar crystals from around her mouth. "We can spend the rest of the day like this," he murmured, "or we can do what I'd planned."

"Mmm, that feels good. What had you planned?"

"Lunch at Treviso, a visit to Murano—where they make all the Venetian glass—then a nap before the big official dinner tonight at Ristorante Ettore, a Vivaldi concert afterward, and a lot of walking and sight-seeing in between."

"Good heavens. It sounds like a lot for one day. Aren't you just the tiniest bit exhausted? I am."

"You mean I've accomplished the impossible—worn you out? If I could crow, I would."

She slapped his cheek lightly. "Men. Always bragging about their prowess."

"If the shoe fits."

"It fits fine, as do a lot of things, and I think we'll drop the subject, thank you, before I turn into a blushing fool." She sat up straight and fluffed up her pillows before leaning back against them. "Oh, except about shoes—I'd love to buy a pair of those soft leather sandals for my sister-in-law. She's pregnant again and her feet are killing her."

"Done. How many nephews and nieces do you have?"

"Let me see. Twelve...no, thirteen. Number fourteen on the way."

"Seriously?"

"Yeah. Family picnics can get kind of crowded. And yes, we always have tacky old fried chicken and potato salad."

"I happen to like fried chicken," he said, "if it's dipped in milk, rolled in rice flakes and fried in sesame oil."

"Wow, that sounds terrific."

How would he react, Matt wondered, to such a huge crowd of relatives? Would he feel invaded? Or would having all that affection and caring and connection fill a hole he'd been carrying around his entire life? It was a sobering yet happy thought and it surprised him with how right it felt.

He turned onto his side and, resting his head on his hand, gazed at her, all soft, round, morning-after femininity. Yes, last night had been a new experience for him, a giving and receiving, a meshing of all his senses that he'd never known before. An emotion startlingly close to joy rose in his throat.

"You've been busy buying presents for your family and I'd like to buy something for you," he said impetuously. "Something very expensive."

"Gee, well, thanks, but it's not necessary."

He stroked the soft skin from her wrist to her elbow. "What would you like?"

"Mmm, not a thing, I mean it."

"But—"

She pressed her fingers over his mouth. "Matt, no gifts," she said more firmly. "This trip is gift enough. And that's the end of the discussion."

She threw back the covers and leaped out of bed. "Last one in the shower has to wash the other's toes."

They spent too much time and too much hot water, but it was a shower to remember. Afterward, very clean and dressed in cool summer clothing for the humid Italian day, they descended the stairs, their arms entwined around each other, and entered the lobby. Signor Mazzeo was on duty at the desk and, upon seeing them, the round man smiled broadly and bid them *Buongiorno*. He then told Matt that there had been a cancellation for the upcoming two nights and would they care to move to a beautiful suite?

Matt translated the manager's offer for Mo, and she looked up at him and tilted her head. "Whatever you'd like, Matt."

"No. I want you to decide."

"Really? Then, I guess you can tell him that I like where we are just fine. In fact, I'm kind of sentimental about that cute little room."

She wrinkled her nose and he gazed down on her shiny, freshly scrubbed face, with that mischievous smile lurking behind her luminous eyes, and he knew he had never felt so lighthearted and carefree in his life. He also knew he was going to kiss her, right there in front of God and the world, and he didn't care who saw.

He did just that, kissed Mo soundly and thoroughly, restraining himself from putting his hands anywhere but on her back and shoulders. Finally, and with great reluctance, Matt tore his mouth away from the kiss and gazed at her. "Any regrets?" he whispered, not sure he wanted to hear the answer. "About last night?"

She kept her eyes on his for a long moment, as though she was looking for messages there. Then she shook her head and offered a small, incredibly sweet smile. "Not a one."

"Whew. Good." He hadn't known he was holding his breath until she answered. He squeezed her shoulders and raised his head to find that he and Mo had an audience, the friendly faces of people who had stopped whatever they were doing to beam their approval. Two Japanese tourists, a gray-haired maid, a boy wheeling a breakfast cart, a workman wearing a tool-filled canvas apron. And Signor Mazzeo, whose expression of warm approval said he took credit for the whole thing. And perhaps, Matt thought, he had the right to do just that.

"Abbiate una piacevole giornata," the manager called out to them, then repeated it in English. "Enjoy the beautiful day."

Matt took Mo's hand and walked with her into the bright sunshine of late morning. Stopping as they hit the street, both of them lifted their faces to the sky, while their hands tightened in unspoken agreement that it was, indeed, a beautiful day.

After they'd walked a while, soaking up the ancient, magical, mystical city, Matt said, "I meant what I said before. About the gift. I would have bought you something and surprised you with it, except I'm not really sure what would please you."

Her cheeks grew rosy. "I think you know that very well."

Chuckling, he threw an arm around her shoulders and hugged her to his chest. "Our tastes are rather different, in case you hadn't noticed. I thought a piece of jewelry, or artwork."

Halting, she disengaged herself from his embrace and stared at him. "But why?"

"So I can watch your face when you pick it out. And, on a less altruistic note, so you'll always remember me and Venice and this time together."

"Is it over already?" She looked alarmed.

"No, no, I didn't mean it to sound like that." He hugged her to him again and kissed the top of her head. They walked on some more, past a shabby but defiantly pink palazzo. "I guess I'm kind of...off-kilter this morning, and things are coming out, well, dramatically."

"Yeah, I'm a little off-kilter, too." She gazed up at him and smiled again, a little shyly, he thought. "Thank you, Matt, you've done plenty already. But you know what? If you really want to watch my face, why don't I go with you and supervise while you buy *yourself* something.''

He stopped and stared at her. "What would I want to buy myself?"

"Clothing, I think. Don't get me wrong, you have wonderful taste, very elegant. But I'd like to see you in something casual. You know, a little less formal."

"I'm not sure they sell shirts with palm trees here in Venice," he said dryly.

"If we looked hard enough, we could probably find one, but, no, I had something else in mind. A lightweight summer suit, I think, like Humphrey Bogart wore in *Casablanca*.''

"I wouldn't even know where to start looking."

"I would."

And so Mo accosted every passing man who wore clothing she admired, and with Matt as translator, got several names of local tailors. When one name was mentioned three times, she smiled triumphantly and said, "Apparently, it's Signor Riccobono. On Via Luana. Goody, we'll put it in the book."

A short water-taxi ride later, Mo found herself in the rear of a small shop, sitting cross-legged on a pile of fabric bolts, while Matt was measured and then fitted for a scrumptious off-white linen suit. She loved watching him in his briefs and T-shirt, loved checking out his arms and chest and legs. He was brown and lean and oh-so-nicely muscled, all over. Especially his buns; the man could have posed for an abs-and-glutes-machine ad. And he'd been hers for an entire night. Lucky, lucky her. She actually sighed aloud, then met Matt's startled glance at her and grinned.

Springing up from the pile of fabrics, Mo played the part of the clucking wife, telling Signor Riccobono a little tighter there, a little more pleat there, then walked slowly around Matt as though she were a designer studying one of her models.

Finally, when the suit was all measured and pinned and draping beautifully over Matt's form, she grabbed a white Borsalino hat from one of the shelves and placed it on his head, tilting it so it dropped rakishly over one eye.

She clapped her hands. "Bravo. Yes, oh, yes. You should be named Giancarlo or Jean-Paul. So continental, so chic, so sexy." She fanned her face with her fingertips exaggeratedly. "Be still my heart."

Matt laughed. "That good, huh? Maybe I should have dressed like this from the beginning. You'd have started panting the moment we got on the plane."

"I *was* panting from the moment we got on the plane."

"Could've fooled me."

"Good. I wanted to."

Arrangements were made to ship the new suit to Budapest, then they went off to a late lunch. They sat in mottled shade on a tree-filled patio and drank mineral water and wine. Mo was starving, for real food, not sweets, for once.

First, they had *bruschetta*—just-picked tomatoes, olive oil with fresh garlic and basil, grilled on thick slices of bread. The taste of the tomatoes was like nothing Mo had ever experienced; closing her eyes, she felt adrift in their sweetness.

"I think I'm starting to get it," she said, then licked some oil from the corners of her mouth.

"If you keep doing that with your tongue, I'll be

forced to take you behind one of those bushes.'' When
she giggled, Matt said, ''You're starting to get what?''

''This taste thing. There are three or four sensations,
one after the other. It's…enticing, isn't it, the way the
garlic flirts with your mouth.''

A slow, pleased look creased his face and he nodded.
''Yes, you're starting to get it.''

The pasta with pesto sauce that followed made her
want to cry with how scrumptious it was. She wondered
briefly if all senses were heightened the morning after a
night like the one she and Matt had just had. Probably,
she thought with contentment. And why not just give in
and enjoy?

''You know, we always talk about my being a food
critic, but we hardly ever discuss you, your career.''

''How many times do I have to say it? I don't have
a 'career.'''

That furrow between his eyebrows made an appearance. ''It seems a waste somehow. You're so intelligent
and have so much energy. If I'd been your father, I
would have insisted that you finish college and come up
with a goal and work toward it.''

''Yes, well, but you're not my father, are you?'' She
was feeling defensive now. Someone as driven as Matt
would have a real hard time understanding a life-style
like hers.

''Besides—'' she decided to try for lightness ''—if
you ever meet my dad, you'll understand how silly that
is. You know that play, *You Can't Take It With You?*
My dad's the guy in the basement who keeps inventing
new fireworks and blowing the place up. Except my dad,
he's always down there creating the next big-selling
kitchen gadget. None of them ever work real well, except once he came up with a way to vacuum the seeds

out of watermelon. Then someone invented seedless watermelon.''

The furrow deepened. ''But don't you miss having a purpose?''

''I have a purpose. To see what's around the next corner.''

''That sounds so...''

''Immature? Aimless? Unsettled?''

He had the grace to look chagrined. ''You've heard those words before.''

''Yeah, and it used to bother me, still does, I guess. It's just that—and you may not be able to understand this—I'm not sure *settled* is such a good thing to be. I change my mind about that a lot. In the meantime, I support myself and have fun. I learn a little bit about the things that interest me, and I meet some wonderful people, and when I think of all the years ahead of me to have more fun and learn more and meet more people, I feel, well, excited. And, you know, I think—I hope—that's an okay way to be. For now, anyway.''

She could see him mulling that over, deciding if he found what she said acceptable. At that moment, Matt was most definitely in his autocratic mode. Really, it was such an ingrained part of him, he would probably always have the tendency.

But he couldn't fool her. She knew what was underneath. It didn't take a genius to see that Matt was a passionate man who'd come to value goals and order because he'd had none as a child, and he squashed down his emotions because no one had ever taken care of him. She felt her eyes filling at the thought of all that need going untended. She looked down at her plate so Matt couldn't see how that sudden insight had moved her.

A soft breeze came up from the canal and made the

leaves overhead rustle. Matt gazed at her for the longest time before shaking his head. "I've never come across anyone like you before."

"And you hope you never will again."

"I'm not sure about that anymore."

A half smile accompanied his answer and Mo said, "Ah-ha, progress. Okay, then let's stop talking about careers and stuff. I mean, here we are, in Venice, for heaven's sake. Who'd have thought it, just—let me see—seven days ago?"

"Eight," he corrected. "Do you know the best time to be here? In February, for the carnival. Everyone dresses in costumes and masks, and there's dancing in the street and a parade. It's a pretty wild time."

"Oh, Matt, it sounds wonderful."

"Maybe we can come back here then."

She looked up at him. He'd said that easily, almost as an afterthought. But was he talking about a future? With her? She shouldn't really read anything more into a casually dropped comment like that, but oh, she wanted to. Maybe the silver-eyed man wasn't her destiny. Maybe Matt was. A little flower of hope started to bud inside her chest. It sprang from the fact that she was in love with him, and the feeling grew by the hour.

Maybe, in time, he could learn to love her. Maybe.

Even though the very mention of the word made him turn colder than a glacier.

13

As Matt followed Mo out of the airport into the terminal, he sensed the change in his mood, from lightness to a grayer, grimmer reality. Too bad, he thought. Prague was a fascinating city, but Matt had been fighting a feeling of—what? gloom—since they'd had their last glimpse of Venice. He really hadn't wanted to leave.

Three incredible days. In that ancient city on the water, he and Mo had had three days in which he'd allowed himself to let go, to get caught up in a mind-melting, body-burning affair. No, not an affair, a romance. It was the only word for it. Romance.

Three days with Mo in a city which cheerfully offered nothing to do except walk, sip coffee, window-shop and ride in a gondola. As he'd written in his notes, when in Venice, one walked, one breathed, one thought, one dreamed.

And, in his case, one made love. With Mo. Often. Astonishing bouts of lovemaking. Afternoon delights in their small room, while the gauze curtains billowed in the breeze from the canal and the sun cast shadows on their naked bodies. More lovemaking in the middle of the night and the early morning. He had taken to it like a parched man at the sight of a waterfall. It had been paradise. The city had worked its spell on him, no doubt about it.

And now it was over.

Ah, well, he thought as he and Mo made their way to a taxi stand at the airport, they would return to Venice together one day.

They? Return together? One day?

Wait a minute, he said to himself. Hold it just one minute.

"Matt? Why are we stopping?"

"Huh? Oh, sorry, I was thinking, uh, about the book."

They walked on, but Matt's mind kept up a furious diatribe. He'd been future-planning with Mo. How could he even allow himself thoughts like that? It must have been a holdover from all the passion and sense of freedom and, yes, sheer happiness, he'd felt in Venice.

All well and good, but Venice was in the past tense.

He had a few more days of travel, a book to write, a career to get on with. It was entertaining, and physically satisfying, having Mo as his travel partner, but there was no way the two of them could survive—together—one day after this trip was over. No way in the world.

The taxi ride took about forty-five minutes, and Mo, with her usual wide-awake verve, kept looking around and commenting about what she saw out the window— groves and groves of trees and fields with women in kerchiefs bent over, tending crops. Once in Prague, they passed stately buildings with soot- and smog-blackened facades, churches with Gothic spires and tall stained-glass windows, clanging trams and small, square automobiles, and houses painted all the colors of the rainbow.

He'd booked them into a hotel in the heart of Wenceslas Square in the New Town section. The building was both run-down and elegant. The honeymoon suite was roomy, with a faded, turn-of-the-century feel to it—delicate furniture with silk-brocade upholstery.

Mo shoved her suitcase into the walk-in closet, then inspected the room, touching everything. "Boy, it's amazing how each city has a completely different character from the one before, huh. Ready to go walking?"

Matt smiled. Mo's delight factor, wherever they were, still operated on all cylinders. "I'm ready."

Taking her hand and tucking it in the crook of his arm, he escorted her down the hall to the antique cage elevator. A few moments later, they were on the streets of Prague.

There were a lot of people and a lot of trees. Also narrow, winding, cobblestoned streets that went up and down hills almost as steep as those in San Francisco. Young people with backpacks and well-dressed women and men strolled by.

"It's a happy city, isn't it?" she said. "People are laughing and talking. How often have you been here?"

"Just once, years ago when the country was still called Czechoslovakia. I've never been to Budapest, by the way."

"Really? Well, good, it'll be one place we can discover together. Until the silver-eyed man shows up, of course," she added lightly.

He stiffened. Had she said that to evoke some kind of jealous response from him?

No, a look at her face told him she'd tossed it off as a joke.

Not that Matt even remotely believed in her *nagyanya's* predictions, but something about Mo's reference to her fantasy future lover made him a little…edgy.

Was he jealous? Absurd, he told himself as they

walked along. It was fatigue. He pushed any other thoughts away as unworthy.

Mo thumbed through a travel book she'd produced from her huge purse. "What shall we see first? The Prague Castle? The Charles Bridge? Oh, look, the Loreto Museum, it has all kinds of fun stuff. Let's go there first."

By late afternoon, Mo and Matt ambled across the Charles Bridge to Old Town Hall, to meet with the photographer. Matt watched Mo's face as they approached the world-famous astronomical clock tower, rising hundreds of feet into the air.

"Wow," she said softly. "Double wow."

"It's something, isn't it?" Matt said.

"Incredible."

Tall and graceful and golden, the huge, intricate clock showed the movements of the sun and moon through the twelve signs of the zodiac.

"Matt, why is the sun going around the earth?"

"The clock's been here since 1490, and they hadn't gotten the news yet that it works the other way around." He slung an arm over her shoulder. "It's almost four—watch what happens on the hour."

Mo watched, feeling like a child waiting for a magic show. As four o'clock struck, she got it. Bells clanged, trapdoors opened and wooden statuettes emerged. Death struck the bells; the Apostles marched past him; a rooster crowed, all in an elaborate mechanical dance.

"It's like a little morality play, huh," she said. "Death is warning about the passage of time, and the rooster is signaling life, and all the other guys telling us to behave along the way."

"That about covers it. They say the clock maker was

blinded by some of the town's big shots, to prevent him from repeating his triumph anywhere else."

"Boy, they really knew how to take care of competition in those days."

He chuckled. "He got them back by plunging his hands into the clock workings, which pretty effectively ended his life—and the clock's too, for a while."

"Yuck."

Out of the corner of her eye, Mo noticed the approach of a tall, very thin man with the saddest face she'd ever seen. In a bass, deeply accented voice, the newcomer said, "Mr. and Mrs. Vining? I am Janusc Kapek. I am here to take the picture."

Mo bit back a smile. The man looked and sounded as if he were informing them of a recent death. He led them around the square, snapping pictures in front of various monuments at a stately pace. When Janusc requested the usual newlywed shot, Mo turned to Matt and clasped her arms around his waist.

She whispered, "This is the first honeymoon picture we've posed for since we've, uh, had carnal knowledge of each other."

"Well, now, I suppose it is. Let's do it up right."

She threw her arms around his neck, then planted her mouth on his. He responded instantly, ferociously, till the two of them were wrapped up in each other and oblivious to everything around them.

Eventually, a low whistle from somewhere made them break the kiss. Dizzy, Mo looked around and remembered where they were. Feeling the heat on her cheeks, she smiled weakly at Janusc.

"A-OK, Mr. and Mrs.," said the photographer solemnly. "I got many good photographs."

As he walked away, Mo glanced up at Matt. It registered then. Something was wrong, had been wrong with Matt's manner all day. Mo's senses had been heightened by their physical intimacy. She was plugged into Matt now in a way that was almost scary; she could feel the slightest change in his mood.

That kiss—it hadn't been in the least bit playful. There had almost been a kind of desperation in it. As though he'd been trying to blot out something dark.

"Matt? Is anything wrong?"

He shook his head. "No. It's just that—it would be nice if a man and woman could sustain the kind of high we had in Venice forever, wouldn't it? But everyone has to come down sometime."

Oh. Was Matt telling her this nice little fairy tale the two of them had been enacting was about to come to an end? Her spirits started to plummet, but she caught herself before they hit bottom.

No, no. Just because Matt said something, or was even feeling something, temporarily, didn't make it so—she had to remember that. She, personally, was not ready to end anything. "I know what will fix that letdown feeling," she said. "Something sweet and disgusting to eat." She smiled at him and took his hand. As they walked away from the square, Mo looked back one more time. "You know what? I think that clock is my favorite sight so far on this trip. I'll always remember it. Something about how it's kept on going all these years, and how beautiful it is."

Which was a funny way to feel, she added silently. Because under that clock, when she and Matt had kissed, she'd felt a different clock ticking, as if they were running out of time.

They sat at the Europa Café with cups of coffee and cream cakes in front of them. Resting her elbow on the table, Mo gazed around the room. The café's interior had remained untouched since its completion in 1912, and the atmosphere of down-at-heel grandeur included a down-at-heel string quartet, playing on a small stage in the corner.

"I feel like I'm in the middle of one of those old black-and-white movies," Mo said. "You know, where all the women wear those slinky gowns and no bra and painted-on eyebrows, and platinum blond hair in tight waves. And all the men dress in white tie and tails every night and everyone is just too too bored? Except I don't own a slinky gown and you're not wearing a tux."

"I didn't bring it with me."

"You actually have one, don't you? Of course you do. And I'll bet it looks great." She cocked her head as she looked at him. "I guess you're the first man I've ever met who actually owns a tux."

"Two, as a matter of fact."

"Why two, for heaven's sake?"

"It was a whim. I couldn't decide between two different styles, and I'd just signed the contract for the radio show and wanted to celebrate."

"So, you celebrated by buying two tuxedos? Weird."

"And four vests. What would you have done?"

Resting her chin in her hand, she thought about it. "Bought presents for everyone I know. Got myself a new car, maybe, or at least a better used one—mine is addicted to gas and is ready for a museum. Let me see. Oh, yes, I would most definitely have hopped on a plane to Europe."

"My two tuxedos were considerably less expensive than all that."

"It does seem that way. I guess it's a good thing I

never have extra money. I'd spend it. Never can seem to hold on to the stuff.''

''Really?''

''You probably balance your checkbook every month. I open a new account every year—it's easier that way.''

He shook his head. ''We are so different, you and I. And I admit it, there are things about you I'll never understand.''

''Or approve of, huh.''

He didn't answer. Instead, he turned in his chair to watch the musicians. Mo studied that classic, brooding profile of his. He was back to judging her again, wasn't he?

But she didn't feel the need to defend herself. She understood now that he went into his judgmental mode when he was hiding from himself, fighting his feelings. Feelings for her? She seriously hoped so. Because he did have them, strong ones—the warmth in his eyes, the touches he gave her, the looks he snuck when he thought she wasn't looking, even the small spurts of jealousy. She hadn't imagined any of that.

However, that didn't mean he would do anything about those feelings. Would he confront them? she wondered. Or let them drain away, like water down a sink?

Maybe she was inventing the whole thing because she wanted him to be feeling all these things. Who knew?

That evening, they attended a Mozart concert in a gorgeous old opera hall—all gold and mosaics and crystal—followed by a late supper at a basement restaurant that descended several stories beneath Old Town Square.

It was a dimly lit medieval stone vault with rough-hewn wooden tables, with a mixed crowd of both Czech and foreign customers. They dined on what Matt told her were traditional dishes of hearty potato soup and beef broth with dumplings. Mo found herself straining to keep the conversation going, and wound up talking too much to fill the silence.

Back at their room, she took a bath in the large old-fashioned claw-footed porcelain tub, and thought about the day. It was time to talk to Matt. Exactly what she would say, she wasn't sure. But things were festering again, and needed airing out.

Wrapping a huge towel around herself, she entered the bedroom. Matt was propped up in bed, making notes.

"I'm not real familiar with Mozart," she said, "or most classical music. Maybe when we get back to San Francisco, I'll take a class."

He glanced up at her, his eyes darkening as he took in her costume, or lack of it. He put his notebook down and held out his arms.

Hmm, Mo thought. Maybe they wouldn't talk, after all.

"You trying to say something, Meester Vinink?"

"I think you started the sentence already. Come here. Now."

"With that kind of masterful invitation, how can a girl resist?"

He pulled her onto the bed, shoved aside her towel and covered her with his body. Soon she was too caught up in the heat to even think about talking things out.

His lovemaking was, as always, inventive and tender, but there was a subtle difference this time. It was serious, almost somber, with no lightness about it in the least. Part of Matt was removed from the act, observing it instead of being totally involved, the way he'd been in Venice.

It scared her. He was pulling away, withdrawing into his shell. And it most definitely was not her imagination.

"Matt?" Mo said afterward, on her side but still enveloped in his arms.

He didn't answer. She angled her head around. He was fast asleep.

She told herself it was natural to pull away. No one could keep up the kind of intensity they'd shared in Italy. Or maybe they'd been together too much and he was feeling tied down. Had she turned into one of those clingy, dependent women because of all the excitement he aroused in her, because of how her emotions were involved?

All right, then, she thought, snuggling back into him in her favorite sleeping position. Dependency she could do something about. If Matt was feeling smothered, she'd take care of that tomorrow.

Matt stared at his toothbrush, shaking his head as he tried to wake up. He was alone in their huge, ornate suite. Mo had risen early, and had been all dressed and ready to leave when he opened his eyes. She'd announced brightly that she was taking off because she needed to be alone to do her exploring thing, and she knew he needed to work on his book.

"See you later," she'd said, and she'd swept out of the room with her usual flurry and bustle.

They'd been here less than twenty hours, and already it looked as if a small tornado had hit her side of the sink. He wondered what it would be like to live with her. Maybe this was one of those compromise areas his married friends talked about, where as long as Mo respected his space, he would have to respect hers. If, of course, they lived together.

Live together? With Mo? What was he thinking?

Matt gripped the sides of the sink and stared into the mirror. Did he actually want to live with Mo? Not only would she be a constant challenge, he'd never lived with a woman before, had never shared dishes, towels, bookcases. He had no idea what that would be like. He and Kay had looked at apartments and figured they'd deal with moving when they returned from their honeymoon. This was an area he knew nothing about.

"Live with Mo?" he said aloud to the bleary-eyed, unshaven man in the mirror. "Together?"

14

Mo threw open the door of the suite. "I did it. I ate carp."

"Carp?"

"Fish. It was terrific. You're always hassling me because I don't eat fish, so I did. Without knowing it. And oh boy, was it good."

She plopped herself down on a gilt-edged chair with spindly legs. Her face glowed with color. She wore one of those pants things that was really a skirt. It was short, too short, Matt thought. Her sleeveless top seemed too skimpy to him, too formfitting. Although he supposed any kind of shirt would look that way on her.

Hold it, he said to himself. Not only was he being a grouch, he was feeling possessive again. He didn't like this mood, didn't like *feeling* any of these things.

"It sounds like you had a great time," he said.

"I did a bunch of exploring, for the book. There's this place that serves blue margaritas, and a vegetarian plate called the Gringo." She pulled her purse onto her lap and started unloading everything onto the floor. "I wrote it all down here somewhere. There was a Cajun restaurant, too, isn't that weird? There was even a sports bar, and I realized I was being a snob—you know, like only Westerners eat Cajun and have sports bars. After all, they might not speak the same language, but people still follow their favorite teams all over the world, and everybody has to eat.''

She found a crumpled piece of paper, glanced at it, then shoved it back into one of the pockets of her purse. ''Now, where did I put that? Oh, and I went to a beer hall, in this kind of arcade right near Old Town Square— lots of wood and those long, long tables…you know, where everyone eats together? And I had a dark beer and some salami and ham. Did you know that Budweiser is a Czech beer? Then they brought out the carp, only they didn't tell me it was carp and it was delicious. Deep-fried and crunchy. Served with this warm potato salad. And the whole thing was only about eight dollars American. So you can put it in the book, you know, for an inexpensive, atmospheric place. Ah-ha. There it is.''

She brought out a torn piece of paper with scribbling on it and handed it to him. It was the top part of a drycleaners ticket for a place in San Francisco.

''Won't you need this?'' Matt asked.

''No, they know me.'' Getting up from her chair, Mo beamed a broad smile at him. ''Matt, you have to come with me. Are you done with your writing? I mean, I don't want to interrupt you or anything.''

Was he done with his writing? What writing? How could he tell her he'd done almost no work on the book? That the day had been filled with mood swings he'd never experienced before. That instead of writing, he'd stared out the window, then gone out for a while, bought her a gift, then suffered all kinds of doubt as to whether or not she'd like it. He'd returned to the room with a lumpy sandwich from a corner shop, and had been at his post at the window ever since, waiting for her to return.

He rose from his chair, determined to shake this

strange, uncharacteristic, downright unfocused state of mind. "Sure, I'll go with you. Where to?"

"It's a hotel."

"But we already have a hotel."

"Not like this one."

As they entered the modest reception area, Mo whispered, "It's owned by nuns, can you believe it? And you don't have to be a nun to stay here, but it helps. Smoking, drinking and staying out after 1:00 a.m. are strictly forbidden."

The building was square and old and not particularly distinctive, at least on that floor. However, Mo told him, in the fifties, it had once housed the secret police.

She led Matt down a flight of stairs and pointed at a row of closed steel doors. "They used to be prison cells, still are, with cots and bars on the windows and everything."

"People stay there?" Matt asked in astonishment.

"Yes. Can you imagine? The nuns have painted them this kind of pink color, but they're still really gloomy."

"Dear God."

She pointed to one of the cells. "P6, that's where President Havel was jailed for a while. It's the most popular room in the place."

Mo took him down one more flight of stairs, one that opened onto a long tunnel. They walked along a chilled, dark underground corridor for several yards until they reached an indentation that led into a cavelike room. Matt could just stand up in the grotto, which he realized was real rock. Its walls dripped with moisture.

"What do you think?" Mo whispered. "Creepy, huh."

Matt was not fond of closed, dark places, and he

didn't care for this one at all. He shivered. "Creepy is the word."

"There used to be skeletons here, one of the sisters told me, from the old days when they tortured people. But not anymore. We hope," she added with a giggle.

Matt started to tell Mo he'd like to leave, but instead, he let out a huge sneeze.

"Bless you," Mo said. "It's soggy down here, huh. You can put this in the book under 'Ex-prison facilities, for that honeymoon with a twist.'"

"Or under 'Places to catch cold so you can have an excuse to stay in bed.'"

"Are you catching cold?"

"I think so." He stepped into a shallow puddle, then shook his foot, annoyed. "I'm sorry, Mo. I'm not feeling adventurous today."

"Scratch one cave exploration."

By the time they got to the restaurant Matt was to review that night, Mo could tell he wasn't well. His skin was pale under his tan, and clammy. And he was as gruff as a bear deprived of hibernating room. This behavior was not unknown to her. One of her brothers was like this; when Patrick got sick, he felt insulted that his body had failed him, and was a cranky, miserable patient.

The restaurant, located in *Stare mesto,* Prague's historic old city, was elegant Art Deco, all polished wood, etched glass and dark marble. Mo and Matt were seated at a window with a view of the Vltava River and Prague Castle, the huge medieval collection of buildings that sat high above the town. Mo wished there were time to go there, but it would have to wait till she returned here. And she would be back, she knew that.

Matt was silent throughout most of the meal. He

seemed to need all his concentration to do his job. Part of her, she was ashamed to admit, felt relieved that he was sick. It might explain some of the last two days' dark mood.

They started with tomato soup, followed by some sort of snail-liver dish the place was famous for. Snail livers? Mo declined to taste it, or the hare salad that followed, which was pronounced by Matt to be decent but not exceptional.

On the other hand, the bread was brown and thickly sliced, very different from French and Italian bread, and she had no trouble eating several slices, slathered with sweet butter.

Mo really worked to cheer Matt up; making her brother laugh had often been an effective way to get him out of his doldrums. She told a couple of terrible jokes, but—like map reading—telling jokes had never been a strength of hers. She usually ruined the punch line.

The entrées were tiny Icelandic shrimp baked with mushrooms, wild boar stew and venison fillets broiled in butter. She actually ate some of all three dishes, telling herself she only had to take a couple of bites and swallow. Matt would be pleased.

For all her sacrifice, he barely seemed to notice. He looked at his food, ate some, made some notes. Period.

Eventually, his mood affected hers and she poked dispiritedly at some of the side dishes—rice and honey, stewed sour cherries, caramelized fennel and roasted potatoes. "These aren't bad," she said to Matt. "Or are they?"

"Not bad, yes."

Oh, dear, Mo thought. Matt, sick, was worse than her brother had ever been. Even the dessert, profiteroles drenched in chocolate sauce, which Mo praised lavishly, declaring she was being corrupted, did nothing to raise his spirits. She decided to stop trying. He was allowed, after all, to be in a bad mood.

The whole meal was too damned heavy, Matt decided, too busy. Besides, he didn't have much of an appetite, which was not a good thing in a food critic. He would have to bend over backward to offer a fair assessment of this restaurant.

On top of that, he was nervous, dammit, because he wanted to present Mo with her gift and he wasn't sure how she would take it. Summoning up whatever fortitude he had left, he signaled the headwaiter to bring the package he'd dropped off earlier. When it arrived, Matt placed it on the table in front of Mo. "Here."

"What's this?"

"Happy Birthday."

"But it's not for two days."

"I know, but I thought while we're in Prague..."

He watched as she tore at the paper around the package with eagerness. "I don't know," he went on. "I just wanted to buy you something and you said I wasn't to buy you anything, but, you know, if it was a birthday gift, well, I assumed you wouldn't refuse."

Why was he babbling this way? He was sounding just like Mo, complete with run-on sentences and all kinds of "you knows" and "wells."

She gasped when she saw the music box—a beautiful miniature of the astronomical clock, complete with statues striking the hour.

"Oh, Matt," she said with tears in her eyes. "Oh, Matt, this is beautiful. Thank you so much."

"You really like it?"

"Like it? I love it."

He exhaled a sigh of relief. "So, then, you're not going to turn it down, even though it is a gift."

"Are you kidding?" she said with a large grin. "Try to take it away from me."

Her smile warmed him momentarily, but then he felt himself sagging. By the time they got to the room, his energy was nonexistent, his headache was pounding and he wanted to bite someone's head off.

With his face still wet from washing it, he threw open the bathroom door and glared at Mo. "Can't you even keep the bathroom clean?"

Mo was unzipping her dress, and he saw her jump at the irritation in his voice. Then she came over to the door, and he could see hurt and anger warring on her face.

"I'm sorry," she said. "I try, really I do. But things just—" she shrugged "—get away from me. I start to clean up, and then something fascinates me, and I get all caught up in that, and then there's no time to go back and make it neat."

Sweeping past him into the bathroom, she pushed all her bottles into one corner, then wiped around the counter with a tissue. "All I've been able to do, over the years, is train myself to keep my mess separate. I haven't touched your stuff, have I? I mean, I've never actually traveled with a man before, not on a trip, so I, well, I'm doing my best." She met his gaze defiantly in the mirror, then bit her lip and looked down. "And I'm running on at the mouth, for a change. Sorry."

He felt ashamed, utterly ashamed. "No, I'm sorry. I shouldn't have said anything. I'm feeling awful, and I'm taking it out on you."

"But you're right."

"No, no. It's okay. Really."

She turned around and faced him, leaning back against the sink and looking up at him with those enormous blue eyes that seemed to ask for a sign of some affection from him. "My gift is beautiful," she said softly, "no matter how you're feeling. It's the best birthday present I've ever had."

What he wanted to do was put his arms around her and bury his head in her soft neck and apologize some more.

But no, he told himself, she would catch his cold. It was better if he made no physical contact with her at all.

"Good," he said, grabbing the towel and wiping his face. "I'm glad."

At another time, Mo thought, it might have been fun to take the night train from Prague to Budapest. But, with these up-and-down bunk beds, and with Matt taking the prize for worst patient in the history of the universe, it wasn't, she decided, the high point of her honeymoon.

She punched in her pillow, which felt as though it were filled with sand and pebbles. This ride wasn't what she'd expected from all she'd heard about intercontinental railroads and watching old Hitchcock movies. This was supposed to be a first-class sleeper, but it was pretty tiny and not at all classy. There was no helpful porter, no drinking water, no dining car, and not even any food machines. And she was practicing self-control rather than utilize the bathroom, which had never heard the word *hygienic*.

Some honeymoon, she thought again.

Stop that, she reminded herself. She wasn't really on an actual honeymoon, even if, up to a couple of days ago, she and Matt had given a pretty good imitation of one.

At any rate, the honeymoon was over. Matt was avoiding her, and she knew deep in her heart it had only a little to do with how sick he felt.

It was a good thing she hadn't told him she loved him, considering how she was pretty sure he wouldn't be real receptive to hearing the news. Even if his feelings for her were as strong as hers were for him, he was fighting them like crazy. And she didn't really want to do battle, not when it came to loving someone.

Still, tomorrow she would be in Budapest, a city she'd been hearing about her whole life. Budapest and the Danube. Mo thought of *Nagyanya* and her predictions. Silliness, of course. After all, who had silver eyes? Gray, maybe, but silver? Ridiculous.

As the train made its way through the countryside, Mo drifted into sleep, keeping one ear out for Matt, should he need her.

Which, of course, even if he did, he'd never admit.

Trains rocking back and forth were supposed to be soothing, but this one was annoying as hell. Matt wished it would stop—his head was killing him. And he was having these strange half thoughts and dreams.

About love.

Love. The word wouldn't stop echoing in his head. Had he ever felt love? he asked himself. For anyone? He must have loved his mother, at least when he was little. Didn't all children love their mothers?

He changed his position. The bed was as small as a child's camp cot. How the hell were people supposed to sleep on these things?

His thoughts drifted. Friends? He had a few. Women? Several in his past. But had he loved?

No, he hadn't felt that particular emotion—if it really existed—for any of them.

He turned over, mopped his forehead with the edge of the coarse cotton sheet and grumbled. He would *not* ask Mo, one more time, for a Kleenex or an aspirin, or mineral water, all of which she packed in that absurd suitcase/purse of hers. He'd been managing alone all his life, dammit, and he could manage to get through a stupid cold without Mo.

But, of course, Mo was why he was thinking about love. He kept pushing the thought away, but it kept coming back with the inevitability of a boomerang. Love.

He wished the word had never been invented.

15

The Budapest station was enormous, with skylights set in very high ceilings. They arrived there at seven in the morning, and for the first time on their trip, Mo put herself in charge of getting them to the hotel. Matt was in bad need of a bed and some sleep—and a doctor, although he refused that suggestion emphatically.

She was pretty sure the taxi driver took the long way around, and she usually wouldn't put up with that, but with all their luggage and a large, sniffling, unhappy man by her side, she figured it wasn't the time to argue about it.

Budapest—actually two cities, Buda and Pest—was a very busy place. Lots of people and cars, charming historical buildings, as soot-covered as Prague's, but not as many. They seemed more uniform somehow, and higher, with tons of windows.

Their hotel was another winner, a great old place which had apparently once been an actual palace. The people who waited on them actually wore uniforms with shiny buttons and epaulets. And the lobby was all brass and chandeliers and Oriental rugs and huge sofas on which were seated all kinds of people in suits with portable phones in their ears. Just like San Francisco.

Their room was the largest one they'd had so far.

Maybe a prince's quarters in the old days, Mo thought. The bed was fitted with thick, feather-filled linens. And the view was spectacular, out over the Danube—the Danube!—and some of the bridges that spanned it, joining the castles of Buda to the market town named Pest.

Mo ordered Matt into the bed and he actually did just that. When she felt his head, it was cooler than it had been on the train, but was still bathed in perspiration.

She called room service and managed to explain she wanted some tea and orange juice sent up, then she tucked his blankets around him and sat on the edge of the mattress. "My dad has a cure for a cold. You down echinacea and goldenseal from the health-food store, a pint of orange juice, two shots of brandy. Then you bundle up like an Eskimo, get under the covers and sleep. One night like that and you sweat it out."

"If you don't die of suffocation. I'll pass. Look, why don't you take off? I hate you seeing me like this."

Biting back a grin, Mo held up her hands to indicate that she was through fussing. A picture formed then, of how Matt must have looked as a little boy, all adorable and furious because he felt helpless and hated it. Her heart went out to him in a mixture of maternal, and definitely not maternal, emotion.

"Well, then, if you're okay, I'll sightsee while you sleep." She kissed his forehead, then smoothed back some of his thick black hair that had stuck to the damp skin. "Get some rest, okay? I love you."

It came out of her mouth just like that.

Automatically. As though she'd said it a hundred times before.

She'd kissed him, then said what she'd been trying not to say for days. Just a simple "I love you."

Not since the night in the gondola had anyone mentioned the *L* word. Usually, Mo blurted out her feelings as they occurred to her, bypassing the judgment part of her head in the process. Holding this one back must have been too much strain.

At any rate, it was out there now.

She held herself still, barely breathing, as she watched Matt's face go from surprise, to something like tenderness, to panic.

The panic was the last thing she saw before he closed his eyes.

His mouth formed two stern lines. He said nothing. Nothing at all. Not one word of reply to the famous three little words.

The son of a bitch.

Slinging her purse over her shoulder, Mo ran out of the room and down the stairs. They were on the twentieth floor, so she got a good workout. When she threw open a door that she thought was to the lobby, she found herself on the mezzanine instead. Before her was a huge breakfast spread—meats and cheeses and breads and fresh fruit and cereals and yogurt. She should have been starving, as they'd last eaten early the evening before, but she'd lost her appetite.

What a surprise. You tell a man you love him and his immediate reaction is to pretend he doesn't hear you, well, you'll probably never want to eat again.

She walked out of the hotel at a fast clip, aware that she was pissed off and probably feeling a bunch of other stuff, too. But after the initial spurt of anger, now she had this incredible blank mind that didn't want to dwell on it. Rejection was like that sometimes. You delayed feeling it as long as you could because it really hurt.

She turned off a main street and found herself in a quiet residential neighborhood. The scent of garlic and onions wafted from a kitchen window. A woman with a brightly colored kerchief tied around her head swept the sidewalk with a homemade broom.

At a small park, men played chess in the shade while a small dog darted through the chestnut trees. She passed huge apartment buildings with courtyards that boasted fruit trees and flower gardens, and where jars of pickled vegetables sat on the sunny window ledges.

At another time she would be rejoicing to be here in the land of her ancestors; she would be exploring, taking it all in with bright curiosity. Instead, she hardly saw any of it. She walked, her mind switched off, disconnected and numb, for what felt like hours. At one point, her stomach rumbled in protest as she passed a line outside a small shop. People were exiting, licking ice-cream cones. Her stomach rumbled again.

Her purse was hurting her shoulder—she should have left it behind, but there'd been no time to unpack it and she'd been in a hurry to escape from Matt. Switching the bag to the other side, she joined the line. She got herself a cinnamon-flavored scoop and thought about how she would tell Matt she'd actually ordered an offbeat ice cream and how proud of her he would be.

And then she remembered that Matt didn't love her; or, at least, had pointedly refused to discuss the subject. The jerk. Being sick didn't mean you got to be unkind. She swallowed down the stab of pain in the back of her throat with soothing ice cream.

Later, much later, it seemed to her, she wound up walking along the banks of the Danube, passing one of the bridges she'd seen from the hotel window. On one side of her was the gray, swiftly moving water; on the other was a huge city street filled with trolley cars, buses and automobiles, and beyond that, a thriving shopping district. She noted both a bagel place and a fast-food restaurant. She smiled sadly at the sight—she couldn't even summon up any enthusiasm for some french fries.

Hugging her arms to her chest, Mo faced the river and stared at a castle in the distance. Castles and palaces and monuments and statues. Museums, parks, theaters, fine restaurants. Planes and boats and trains. What a lot she and Matt had packed into this trip.

This "honeymoon" trip.

The hurt, dark and salty, rose again in the back of her throat. Tears flooded her eyes. Darn it, why did she always have to cry? She reached into her purse for some Kleenex. Did she have any left after last night on the train? She was pretty sure she had a little travel pack somewhere in there.

Mo set the bag down on the concrete sidewalk and started to unload everything in it. Socks, matchbooks and ashtrays, a bottle of water, part of a muffin, a paper fan, a plastic rain kerchief. Stuff and more stuff.

Somewhere behind her, she sensed a presence, but before she could turn around, her purse had been snatched up and a teenage kid was running off with it.

"Hey!" she called out.

Someone else shouted a word she didn't know and then she saw a man with dark sunglasses and a mustache take off in pursuit of the thief. Mo was about to go after both of them, when, twenty yards ahead, the second man attacked the kid who'd lifted her purse. There was a brief scuffle, then the thief ran away, and the man with the sunglasses and mustache trotted back to her with her purse in his hand and a huge grin on his swarthy face.

As he got closer, she noted the dark, curly hair and the printed bandanna worn across his forehead. He wore a torn T-shirt and jeans and seemed to be about her age.

Not too tall, but kind of cute. His impudent grin reminded her of Kevin Kline. She liked her purse's rescuer immediately.

Gypsies were Hungary's largest minority, and Mo was pretty sure one of those fascinating people was standing in front of her right this minute.

With a nod of his head and that charming smile, her hero offered her purse to her, saying something she couldn't understand.

She accepted the bag and slung it over her shoulder again, saying, *"Koszonom szepen,"* which meant thank you. It was one of the ten or so phrases *Nagyanya* had taught her.

More excited sentences tumbled from the man's mouth, but, laughing, Mo shook her head. *"Nem, nem,"* she said. "No, no. I don't speak Hungarian."

He switched to another language and she wondered if it was Romany, the international language of Gypsies. Not that she understood that one any better. Again, she shook her head sadly. "Sorry. No."

He looked disappointed, but in the next moment brightened up. Holding his finger in the air to indicate she should wait a minute, he went over to a small wooden cart by the side of the road. She hadn't noticed it before. It was crudely made and painted white. There were bunches of flowers on the cart, some in paper, some in vases. They weren't particularly fresh, but they were colorful.

Mo figured the cart belonged to the man. He perused his collection, then chose a bunch of mixed blooms—daffodils and daisies and a couple of tall, white blossoms that Mo didn't know the name of. Coming toward her again, he bowed from the waist and presented her with the bouquet.

She nodded, saying, *"Koszonom szepen"* again and taking the flowers from him. They stood looking at each other for a silent minute. Then he did a little soft-shoe step and she did one back, and they both laughed.

The man began to hum a song that had a waltz rhythm, then he swayed to the beat. How wonderful, Mo thought, her body moving automatically in time to the music. Just what she needed to brighten her day. A dancing man on the banks of the Danube.

Singing now in a loud, robust voice, the flower seller held out his arms to indicate she should join him. She didn't even have to think about it; after all, why not? Why not put away all thoughts of the grumpy man lying in bed back in the hotel, and give herself up to a little moment of gaiety?

As she drifted closer to the flower seller, he pushed his sunglasses up onto the top of his head and, laughing, reached for her.

Mo stopped dead in her tracks, her hands against his chest. She stared. Hard.

His eyes. They were…gray? No, not gray.

Grabbing him by the shoulders, Mo pulled him around so that he was facing the sun, and stared again into his eyes. No doubt about it. The very same color of the tea set that sat on her mother's sideboard at home. After it had been polished to gleaming.

16

—————

Matt lowered himself onto the bench and rubbed his face with his hand. Why was he here? How big a fool would he seem to Mo, if he ever found her? She could be anywhere in the city, anywhere at all, probably slipping on a puddle or kicking up some kind of turmoil, from which she would extricate herself, somehow, intact. She certainly didn't need him to rescue her, or to even lay eyes on him, probably.

Two hours earlier, he'd been lying in the hotel bed, restless and feverish. He was pretty sure that all he had was a cold, but it seemed to drain his energy. He kept drifting in and out of sleep, but he remembered indulging in pop psychology by wondering if his illness was more emotional than physical. Was his body reflecting the war raging in his head? Did that kind of thing really happen? Whatever the answer, he had still felt pretty bad.

Suddenly, he sat up straight in bed, a sense of panic overtaking him. Mo had told him she loved him! And like some prizewinning idiot, he'd been so thrown by her admission, he'd clammed up. By the time he'd recovered his wits enough to say something—anything— she'd hightailed it out the door.

But where had she gone? Mo. He had to find Mo.

He'd risen from bed, thrown on some pants and a shirt and had gone out looking for her. No luck. So here he was, on a bench near the Danube, at a loss for what to do next. His gaze swept the gray, fast-moving river, the picturesque hills on the opposite shore, and finally rested on the sight of something in the distance, half a football field away. Two people. Mo?

And who was that with her? A dark-haired man near a flower cart? Matt half rose from his bench, thinking he would make his way over there and— Then what? What would he say to her? What was he prepared to say?

He sank back down, his gaze fixed on the scene farther down the riverbank. Mo and the stranger seemed to be laughing and having a great old time. Then they both began swaying and laughing some more; Matt felt his back teeth clench at the sight.

Then the stranger held out his arms to Mo and, still swaying, she walked toward him. But she stopped. Even at this distance, Matt could tell she was startled by something. He watched as she turned the stranger into the sun and stared into his eyes.

No, Matt thought. Not his eyes.

But yes, Mo gazed, astonished, into the stranger's eyes and no one had to tell Matt what color they were.

He felt as though someone had gut-punched him, as though all the oxygen had been whisked out of him. He slumped against the seat and held his head in his hands. So this was how it felt. To finally want something badly and at the point of admitting it to yourself, have it snatched away from you. His heart hurt. He'd heard the expression all his life, but he'd never known what it meant. But this was how pain felt, this was the cost of caring deeply about someone.

The cost of loving. There, he'd said it. To himself, anyway. And about two hours too late.

He forced himself to get up from the bench and, walking in the opposite direction of Mo and the stranger, made his way back to the hotel.

He was under the covers when Mo returned an hour later. What had she been doing all that time? He couldn't bear the direction of his thoughts. Through half-closed lids he noted that she seemed subdued. She came to the bed and stood over him, but he didn't look at her.

"Matt?" he heard her say.

"Hmm?"

He felt the mattress sag as she sat next to him and put her hand on his forehead. "You're cooler now. How do you feel?"

He shrugged. Again, he had no words, none at all.

"I found out that Budapest is famous for Turkish baths. They have this real ornate setup at the Hotel Gellert a couple of blocks away, and I went there to check it out." She spoke quickly but without her usual animation, which sounded strange to him. She'd been to a hotel? He hated that.

"Maybe it would be good for you to go there," she went on. "It's huge, lots of pools and steam rooms, and the ladies who give massages could be weight lifters. We could put it in the book. What do you think? Would you like to go?"

He shook his head and murmured, "Just sleep."

"All right. We need to cancel the restaurant tonight."

"No. I have to go," he mumbled. "Don't have a choice. It's not till ten, so I'll be better by then."

He heard her sigh softly. "Okay. Go to sleep then."

"Where are you going?"

He wondered if his fear showed in his voice, but he

was able to relax a little when she said, "Nowhere. I'll be right here."

And then he sought the oblivion of sleep.

The restaurant was located on the riverbank, just across the Margaret Bridge. Mo and Matt were seated on the upper outdoor terrace; colorfully costumed folk dancers performed on the level below. The waiters and waitresses wore traditional Hungarian peasant clothing. Mo liked the place because it was the least formal of all the official restaurants they'd eaten in on the trip.

Staring around the room at soft lighting and flickering candles on the tables, Mo felt strangely calm, and more than a little sad. Her grandmother had only got part of the prediction right. The flower seller might have had the right color eyes, but nothing else had been right. Her pulse had remained steady, there'd been no sizzling connection between them. The silver-eyed man wasn't the one for her.

Nor was Matt, apparently. Her anger at him had completely dried up as she'd watched him sleep away the rest of the afternoon. Instead, there had come a gentle sadness, which she wasn't used to feeling, and an inner stillness, which was most definitely uncharted territory.

When Matt woke up, he was even more remote than before. As they'd dressed for the evening—him in his new white suit, which, sick or not, looked deliciously continental on him; it was as though he were occupying a different planet. The two of them had barely talked on the way here. Mo wondered how a trip that had started out in such high spirits could finish on such a downer.

She also wondered if she'd ever smile again. She sure didn't feel like it tonight.

"I wonder where the photographer is," Matt said, looking around the restaurant. "He's meeting us here."

Mo shrugged and took a sip of wine. "Beats me."

He turned his attention back to her, gazed at her for a moment, then frowned. Uh-oh, she thought. What's the matter now?

"I need to ask you a favor," Matt said.

"A favor? What?"

"One of the side effects of a cold is stuffed nasal passages, which affects your sense of smell, which affects your sense of taste. So, I can't taste anything."

"Wow. Major problem, I guess."

"So, will you describe the tastes to me? As best you can?"

"Really? You trust me?"

"Yes, Mo. I guess I do."

Paprika, Hungary's famous red powder ground from peppers, seemed to permeate a lot of the dishes. First there was *babgulyas,* a hearty bean soup and *halaszle,* a fish soup. Mo described the first as thick and peppery, and the second as way too fishy. Matt made notes in his book.

For the main courses there were chicken paprikash with pasta dumplings; *toltott kaposzta*—whole cabbage leaves stuffed with rice, meat and spices; a combination platter including roast goose leg, goose cracklings and goose liver; and something called Szinbad's Favorite— pork stuffed with chicken liver, rolled in bacon and served in a paprika and mushroom sauce.

"Uh, this one," Mo said, chewing thoughtfully, "the chicken, it kind of hits the roof of your mouth like one of those red-hots, you know those little candies? Mixed with chicken soup."

"Red-hots and chicken soup," Matt repeated as he wrote it down.

"And this goose—well, it's kind of like well-done chicken, only saltier and tougher, you know, like a leather vest."

"Salty leather vest."

"This pork thing, it's got enough flavors to last a lifetime, but I really can't come up with the words. Spicy, I guess, and sweet and kind of greasy. Like bacon and goop."

Matt looked up from his notes and considered her. "Maybe we'd better forget it."

"Sorry. I don't know spice names and all that subtle stuff you do."

"Why should you? It's not your field."

She felt herself stiffening. Matt might be under the weather, but she wouldn't stand still for a barbed comment about her lack of direction. "I don't have a field, remember?"

"Yes, you do." He smiled, but it was more bittersweet than amused. "Your field is life, Mo, and the living of it. I envy you."

"Excuse me? You what?"

"I wish, part of me wishes, that is," he amended, "that I was more like you."

"You do?" Where had this come from? she wondered.

"Yes. Listen, Mo, I need to—"

Whatever Matt was about to say was thwarted by a Gypsy violinist who had been entertaining the other diners and who now swept up to their table. Short and stocky, nearly bald, and dressed in all his embroidered finery, he favored them with a broad, gold-toothed grin.

With a flourish of his bow, he began to play a very sad, very romantic melody.

Mo's attention was drawn to the musician; something about his song reflected an ache deep in her soul. Her head moved in time to the music. The Gypsy's bow moved smoothly over the strings, and she watched his hands for a while. When she caught a glimpse of the watch on his wrist, she noticed that it said eleven-fifty. In ten minutes, she would be twenty-eight. So what? Shaking her head, she smiled cheerlessly to herself.

"What are you thinking about?" Matt asked.

She glanced over at him and shrugged. "My upcoming birthday."

"Birthday?" said the violinist. He stopped his recital right in the middle, made a loud announcement in flowery Hungarian and began to play the Happy Birthday song.

Mo blushed as all the other diners joined in, with expansive smiles on their faces, in a language that was vaguely familiar from years spent on the lap of a woman she'd loved very much. Mo wished she could be happy about being born, but this evening it wasn't up there on her gratitude list.

After everyone had applauded, and Mo was wiping one lone tear from the corner of her eye, Matt said, "Mo?"

Now the violinist was joined by a dramatic-looking, dark-haired woman with large earrings and bangle bracelets; she began to sing an even more mournful song than the previous one, a wistful melody filled with suffering. Mo stared at the singer. Woman to woman. The singer obviously knew just what Mo was feeling.

Matt felt his jaw tightening. He was starting to get irritated. No, in truth, he was starting to panic. He went for it one more time. "Listen, Mo, I need to talk to you, to tell you something."

"I'll accept Happy Birthday."

"No, I mean it. There's something upsetting…no, difficult for me to say."

Turning toward him, she put her hand over her heart and looked at him anxiously. "What? You're scaring me."

"I didn't mean to." He was doing this all wrong. Where was Matthew Vining, glib radio personality, when he was really needed? "It's about what you said today."

"Today?"

"Earlier, in the room."

"You mean, about my dad's cure for a cold?"

"No, after that." Damn, this was hard.

"Is this Twenty Questions or something?"

"No. Dammit, about when you told me you loved me."

He saw her go very still. She could have been a statue except for the blinking of her eyelashes.

"What I want to say… I mean, the thing is—" He put his hand over hers and squeezed. She *had* to listen to him. "Mo. Please, don't go off with him."

"Don't go off with who?"

"That man. The one with silver eyes. I mean, he's a flower seller. Which, don't get me wrong, is probably a perfectly honorable living; but you don't know him. Mo, you don't even speak the same language—"

"How do you know about the flower seller?"

"I saw the two of you today."

"You followed me? But why?"

"That's not important. What is important, crucial, really, is that you understand that— The thing is— Dammit, Mo, I couldn't bear it if you left me.''

''But I wasn't going—'' As his last words registered, she stopped talking. She stared wide-eyed at him, a statue again, and for one of the few times in her life, Matt imagined, speechless. The music played on, but their gazes remained locked for many heartbeats.

''Are you going to say anything?'' he asked her, really worried now.

She shook her head slowly and seemed to come awake. ''You're doing just fine.''

The violinist and the singer must have sensed the drama going on at their table because the two of them moved in even closer, one on each side of the table, and began another heartrending lament.

Mo glanced at each of the musicians, smiled quickly, then turned her attention back to Matt. Keeping one hand under his, she leaned on the table, rested her chin on her other hand and gazed at him with a small, encouraging smile. ''So. You were saying?''

''I haven't cried since I was a little boy and I had to give away my puppy because my mother's new husband was allergic to animals, but I feel as though I could cry right now at the thought of losing you.''

Mo let out a gasp, unbearably moved. She clutched Matt's hand even harder as her own eyes filled. ''Oh, God, that's so sad,'' she said, then burst into tears herself.

The dark-haired singer, seeing all the weeping at the table, crossed her hands over her heart and turned up the throbbing emotion in her song.

Through the haze of her tears, Mo watched Matt's shimmering eyes gazing at her. At this moment, he was the direct opposite of distanced, and all because he feared losing her. Her heart took off, on the wing, out of sight. It was glorious.

She gazed into Matt's soulful, brimming eyes and started to speak. Just then, the singer's bracelets caught the light from the candle, the reflection making Matt's tears shimmer. Which made his eyes shimmer. Which made his eyes...

Silver.

That brought another gasp, then more sobbing from Mo, a river of salt water, all the way down her cheek and onto her neck. Matt picked up a napkin and dabbed under her lids and around her collarbone. "You are so lovely," he said as though bewitched.

"But—" Mo's throat closed up.

"What?" he said. "Tell me what you want to say."

She sniffled a little bit more, grabbed the napkin and blew into it. "Oh, Matt."

"Yes."

"Your eyes—they're silver."

"Excuse me?"

"I mean, with the candle and the tears, they're silver. Get it? Here we are on the banks of the Danube, moments before my twenty-ninth year is about to start, and you are a man with silver eyes. Tell me now how absurd my *nagyanya* was."

She saw the light dawn on Matt's face. His expression of awe made him seem years younger, totally lacking in cynicism, as though he'd witnessed a miracle. He took the edge of the tablecloth and wiped some mascara from under her lower lids.

"Can't take you anywhere," he said in a voice as warm and adoring as she could have hoped for in any of her fantasies.

They sat and smiled stupid smiles at each other, totally

oblivious to the quiet murmur of the other diners, the sounds of violin and song, the quick breeze fluttering the candlelight at all the tables. Somewhere far away a clock sounded. Twelve slow strokes signaled the hour of midnight.

"Happy Birthday," Matt whispered. "And, in case you can't tell, I love you. It hurts how much I love you."

"I'm going to cry again."

He kissed her hand and held it tightly. "Weep away. I can handle it. And I want to apologize for snapping at you. You didn't deserve it. You're wonderful."

"So are you," she said, sniffling.

As though on cue, they both rose at the same time and leaned over the table. He framed her face with his hands, and they kissed.

"Ahem," Mo heard, then "Ahem" again. Reluctantly, she and Matt separated.

A paunchy man in an ill-fitting gray suit stood next to them, mopping his forehead with a large white handkerchief. "I am so sorry," he said. "My car, it is a disaster. I am late. Please forgive me."

"For what?" Mo asked.

"I am the photographer." He looked from one to the other. "I am to take pictures." When she and Matt continued to stare blankly at him, he said, "I am, am I not, talking to Mr. and Mrs. Matthew Vining?"

Matt turned to Mo and winked, then faced the photographer again, with a poker face. "Not really," he said, "but we're getting there."

Epilogue

As they were going through Customs at San Francisco International Airport, Matt watched while Mo explained to the Customs inspector, very sweetly, what all her purchases were and who they were for and how much they cost, even though she couldn't seem to find the receipts and how she knew they were here somewhere, if he would just be patient while she looked through her purse, until the official gazed at the heavens, muttered something under his breath and let her through without a penalty.

Mo slung her huge purse onto the cart Matt had rented, and, arm in arm, they came through the Arrivals gate just in time for homecoming pictures. As the photographer, a slim young man in a loud polka-dot shirt, danced around them, directing them in various poses, Matt said to Mo, "You know, I think I've figured you out."

"Let me in on it, so we'll both know."

"You seem scattered and mercurial, but underneath, I suspect, you're a rock."

She threw her arms around his neck. "And you, beneath that controlling, orderly exterior beats the heart of a marshmallow."

"Marshmallow?"

"Marshmallow."

"Well, this marshmallow loves you."

"And this rock loves you." Their kiss drew exclamations of approval from the photographer, who asked for another one.

"First," Matt said to Mo, pulling her body even more tightly to his, "I propose we travel some more together, dine a lot and make love all the time."

"Sounds like a plan."

"You could even have a field of expertise."

"We starting on that again?"

"No, listen. You could be a travel expert. You have all the makings of a great one, trust me. You could be a guest on my show...or we could have a show together!"

Mo leaned back and eyed him dubiously. Why did she suddenly feel as though they'd changed places? "Uh, Matt, aren't you getting a little carried away?"

"No. Listen. 'Dining With Vining' could be changed to 'The Matt and Mo Show.'"

"Excuse me?" she said, raising one eyebrow sardonically.

"Okay," Matt said graciously, "'The Mo and Matt Show.'"

Grinning, Mo shook her head. The man of her dreams was right here, right now, not silver-eyed on the Danube, but brown-eyed and in America. And dear, sweet *Nagyanya* had made it all happen. *Koszonom szepen*, she whispered silently to her grandmother. Thank you.

Aloud, she said, "Nah. You can have top billing, just as long as I can have you." She stood on tiptoe to kiss him soundly. "'The Matt and Mo Show' it is."

* * * * *

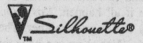

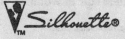